BLUESKY AND SUNSHINE
Song of Life – Book 1

Tony Chandler

BLUESKY AND SUNSHINE
Song of Life – Book 1

DOUBLE DRAGON

Dedication

For Melva

Tony Chandler

Chapter One

A brilliant shaft of light flashed through the trees and announced the long-awaited appearance of the sun.

The birds sang out in celebration.

The early birds had been singing for almost an hour with the first hint of the brightening horizon. As the stars faded one by one and the sky transformed from velvety blackness to pale blue, more birds awakened and joined their voices to the chorus.

But as the golden rays multiplied, the melodic phrases and twinkling trills took on a real urgency. Birds sang out from every direction and increased their volume ten-fold when the blinding orb of the sun revealed itself at last through the leafy canopy.

A new day began exactly as every other day -- and yet as unique as an individual snowflake.

The sun's golden light gleamed across a street named Willow Hollow and into the yard behind the house located at number 3477. A particularly bright beam pierced through the leafy canopy of a dogwood tree and lit up a single branch like a spotlight. Two mockingbirds sat on the branch and waited expectantly as three eggs shuddered with life.

And in that very moment, the miracle of birth occurred.

Small chunks of eggshell cracked and fell away from one egg as it rocked excitedly. A tiny voice called out with heartwarming urgency as the outside world became visible for the very first time.

Sunshine's heart quivered with excitement.

The female mockingbird cocked her head to one side and peered intently. She flicked her long, graceful tail as her excitement reached a fever pitch. She then hopped from side to side and opened her beak in a smile.

Sunshine couldn't contain her emotions any longer. She stretched out her wings and held them out wide. With her face toward the sky, she sang her happiness for the entire world to hear.

Suddenly, the egg rocked side to side as more eggshell crumbled away. Seconds later, a tiny beak and face peeped out.

The first baby emerged from the shell.

The two lifelong mates stared with open beaks as the tiny form pushed the remaining section of eggshell back and wriggled itself free.

The fragile creature shuddered with the first brush of air across its wet body. Its head seemed far too large compared to its tiny body in that first minute of life outside the egg. Struggling to lift its head and discover its new surroundings, the baby moved with jerky, unwieldy motions as it used its muscles for the first time.

Both parents leaned closer with eager expectation.

Lifting its head up, the baby cried out its first, precious words.

"I'm cold, and I'm hungry!"

Sunshine turned to her mate and laughed out

loud.

Treetop smiled and flicked his long tail proudly.

"Feed me! Feed me! Feed me!" the baby mockingbird peeped urgently.

"Oh, Treetop. It's a little male. And he looks just like you," Sunshine trilled happily.

Treetop sang out joyfully as he leapt into the air and flew far above the trees, his song filling the air.

The birds in the nearby trees stopped their own singing to listen with awe and respect, realizing that a proud new parent was singing about the birth of his babies. Treetop's vibrant voice echoed throughout the trees.

As the golden sun rose steadily into the clear blue sky, the other two babies slowly worked their way free.

Three newborn babies now cried out to their parents with constant calls for attention.

Sunshine and Treetop got to work.

First, Treetop reached into the nest and picked up the largest empty eggshell with his beak. He leapt into the air with it and then flew far away from the nest before he dropped the eggshell into the middle of a large bush.

He quickly flew back to the nest to remove more egg debris.

While he and Sunshine flew back and forth and carefully cleaned the nest, they recalled the two oldest sayings of nest-wisdom that all families of bird held dear.

The first: '*A clean nest means a clean bird.*'

This oldest bit of wisdom applied first for the

9

parents as they sat long hours warming the eggs before the young hatch. But its primary meaning applied to the parents after the young hatched -- keeping the young clean and quickly disposing of all waste, external and internal.

Of course, caring parents by and large kept the nest and the babies clean; it was simply a part of being a good parent. But keeping a nest clean was not just important for appearances; it was an essential part of protecting the babies from potential predators. Snakes, possums, raccoons, and other birds would relish a meal of tender babies if they could find the nest hidden among the leaves.

If parents allowed waste to fall to the ground directly underneath the nest, they might return to the chilling sight of an empty nest and a few scattered feathers -- and no babies.

The second proverb had a similar meaning, but it applied more broadly to the everyday life of all birds. On any given day and in any given tree, a bird would likely hear this bit of wisdom chirped and chided by a parent to its offspring …

'*A stupid bird fouls its own nest.*'

Treetop and Sunshine had been mates four seasons now. Together, they had successfully raised six sets of young. Their first nestlings usually hatched in early spring. After these babies were taught how to fly and how to feed using their own skills, Treetop and Sunshine would build another nest and raise another set of young, these usually being born during the heart of the summer.

The babies born in the nest this bright,

wonderful day were their second set of hatchlings this season.

Sunshine flew back to the dogwood tree to feed her babies for the first time. Their cries for food touched her heart and urged her to fly faster.

But as she approached, Treetop glanced up at her with a strange expression, and she felt her heart seize with dread.

"There's a problem," he said simply.

"What's the matter?" she asked with a frantic tone.

"Something's wrong."

"What? What is it?" Sunshine gripped the branch tightly.

"It's... it's one of the babies."

"What is it? Tell me!"

But Treetop turned away and shook his head.

"Tell me!" she pleaded urgently.

Treetop sighed heavily. He spoke with his back still turned. "He's deformed."

Those two, heart-rending words started ringing inside her head in a nightmarish chant -- over and over again. The chant quickly drained all her energy and then all her joy. Her legs grew weak while the world around her spun out of control.

'*He's deformed...*'

She had never considered this possibility.

Somewhere deep inside her breast, where her heart had beat so happily a moment before, a dark and terrible emptiness began to blossom like a cancer.

"Feed me!"

Sunshine looked away in horror.

She was afraid to look.

But she was afraid not to look.

Sunshine took a deep, shaky breath.

And turned around.

Three baby mockingbirds lay sprawled in the bottom of the nest seemingly naked with their fine down clinging to their fragile bodies in wet, dark streaks. The wet down would soon dry and give their tiny bodies some protection from the air.

Sunshine leaned forward, carefully looking over each baby in turn and trying to determine what was wrong, but all she could see were three tiny babies who shuddered with new life.

She turned to her mate.

"They look fine to me," Sunshine said with a rush of hope.

"He's deformed." Treetop groaned. He nodded at the nest. "The little one -- the last one born. Look closely."

Sunshine's head spun as she realized the littlest baby was moving oddly. And the more she looked, the odder his struggles seemed.

"Look at him closely," her mate added with anguish.

Hot tears clouded her vision as she tried to focus.

Without intending to, she looked at the first-born male instead. The baby noticed his mother's glance and cried out once again, his message direct and to the point.

"Feed me! Feed me!"

12

Sunshine ignored the cry even though it tugged at her heart and triggered something deep inside. She looked him over carefully, blinking back her tears.

Next, she looked at the second born, a female. The baby recognized her mother and cried out with the same, urgent message. She smiled down at her daughter a moment.

Finally, after a long and fearful hesitation, she turned to the last born, another male.

The baby struggled to raise himself up with open beak in expectation of his first meal.

But this baby had more trouble than the others and could not balance himself enough to lift his head upright. The other two had successfully raised their heads with beaks open as they pleaded urgently to be fed.

The last baby struggled awkwardly...

He wobbled unsteadily a moment and fell backward with a plop.

Sunshine couldn't understand why he couldn't raise himself up like the others. She looked closer and gasped.

"He only has one leg!"

Treetop and Sunshine looked at each other with great sadness in their eyes.

The terrible emptiness inside her breast smothered Sunshine. She felt like she was suffocating from the overwhelming sadness. It felt as if her world were crumbling around her.

"It can't be..." she whispered.

"He's... he's deformed" Treetop collapsed on

13

the branch and sat there shaking his head.

Sunshine felt the world spinning out of control.

"He's only got one leg," Treetop repeated in a whisper. He began to sob silently.

Sunshine peered down at the struggling baby, who'd finally managed to raise his body partway up on his one leg. She looked closer and saw only a tiny stump where the second leg should have been.

She stared at the baby a long time in stunned silence.

She felt helpless. She felt powerless. And she didn't know what to do.

Treetop hopped up beside Sunshine as all three babies suddenly cried in unison and begged to be fed.

"He'll never live," Treetop said sadly. "He'll never live long enough to leave the nest."

"What? How can you say such a thing?" Sunshine asked haltingly. Her mind was in so much turmoil, it seemed everything was confusion.

"Have you ever seen a one-legged mockingbird?" Treetop asked.

"I don't know..." Sunshine whispered with doubt. "I'm not sure..."

"I mean, have you ever met a one-legged mockingbird? Have you even heard of one?" Treetop asked more forcefully.

Sunshine quickly looked away as more hot tears streamed down her cheeks. After a moment, she looked back at her babies. She focused on the poor one-legged baby while her heart broke in two.

"No, I've never heard of a one-legged bird

before…"

Chapter Two

"Good morning, Sunshine."

Sunshine's eyes fluttered open as she awakened to a new day.

Instantly, the overwhelming sadness from yesterday flooded her mind and heart. Now a terrible ache filled her breast -- where once her heart had been so happy.

She looked up at her mate with puzzlement and wondered how he could act so... normal? How could he awaken her as if nothing had happened?

How could he just stand there when one of their babies was going to die?

"Are you all right?" Treetop asked with concern. He hopped up on the branch just above the nest.

Sunshine rested on the nest, her warmth protecting the babies underneath her feathers. She felt one of the babies wriggle with life.

She shuddered and wondered if it was the deformed baby moving under her.

"Yes, yes. I slept really deeply last night," she lied, not daring to tell him of the disturbing dreams that had haunted her all night long. "I didn't know where I was when I woke up just now. It just kind of... scared me."

Treetop chuckled lightly. "Well, you're sitting on the same nest you've sat on each night for over two weeks, except now three babies lie underneath you."

Sunshine's dark, slender beak, curved slightly downward like all mockingbirds. Now she opened it ever so slightly in a bird-smile at the thought of their three babies, but the expression in her piercing eyes remained somber.

"Are you sure everything is all right?" Treetop asked again.

They looked deep into each other's eyes a long moment in mutual silence.

She slowly stood up and glanced back down under her feathers.

The three tiny forms lay motionless except for their regular breathing. Their soft down had now dried and covered their bodies like a fine layer of gray fleece. Though their large eyelids remained tightly shut, their heads jerked ever so slightly when the cool morning air washed across their tiny bodies.

"Sit on them until they wake, please." Sunshine hopped onto a branch on the opposite side of the nest from Treetop. "Do you have breakfast for them?"

Treetop stepped into the nest, carefully placing his three-toed feet between the sleeping forms. Before he sat down, he fluffed out his feathers to provide them comfort and warmth.

"I found several juicy bugs. I'm digesting them right now. Breakfast should be ready in a few minutes when they awake!"

Sunshine nodded approvingly, although in her heart she again felt terrible confusion. They were both talking as if nothing had happened.

17

"Good, good. I'll go get myself some breakfast and then eat a few more bugs for the babies. I should be back shortly."

"Good hunting!" Treetop whispered enthusiastically while he gently moved his body from side to side to nestle the babies deeper within the warmth of his feathers.

She leapt into the air and experienced the refreshing rush of wind against her face. She performed a quick check of the sky and nearby trees for signs of predators who might be watching for hints of parents feeding newborn babies. Sunshine hadn't raised fifteen babies without learning to be vigilant. She'd not lost a single baby to predators yet, or due to anything else for that matter, and she wasn't about to start now.

But predators were an especially grave danger.

Last season, she and Treetop had been forced to fight off a gang of Blue Jays who stumbled upon their nest. It had been simple coincidence, the jays landing in their nest tree. Of course, the jays had immediately heard the cries of the helpless babies.

The ensuing battle had been fierce. Treetop took on three of the biggest birds by himself while she took on the other two. Both parents fought with a vengeance, diving at the jays and then going into a tight turn and attacking from a different direction. The air had reverberated with their angry cries while they pressed their attacks.

The gang were quickly confused by the overwhelming intensity of the parent's assaults. Still, the Blue Jays outnumbered the Mockingbirds and they regrouped and fought back with beak and claws. The melee quickly grew to a fever pitch.

But the ferocious attacks of the parents prevailed and they drove the jays off in raucous retreat. And though Treetop and Sunshine had both been bruised and each missing a few feathers, the gang had never come close to their precious babies.

After assuring herself that all was safe, she soared away from their tree. The exhilaration of flight sent a thrill throughout her being. Her heart pounded with excitement, and she relished this welcome emotion that quickly pushed aside the suffocating sadness.

Flying had never felt so good.

She flew faster. The thrill of her newfound freedom filled her heart with gladness.

As her wings beat rhythmically and the distance grew greater, she felt a sense of relief -- almost as if she were leaving all her troubles behind.

Like all mockingbirds, her lithe body was covered by light gray feathers across her back, head and down to the base of her long tail. Her breast and belly area was adorned with whitish feathers. Each time she fully extended her wings in flight, the famous 'white patch' flashed like an insignia on her mid-wing. Her long, elegant tail feathers were black with several white feathers on each edge that also flashed while in full flight.

Her fears faded, and she slowed her wing strokes.

Sunshine now flapped her wings several times and then folded them against her body, allowing her to drop in a slow arc through the air. After a few seconds, she flapped her wings again until she regained her original altitude; then she again folded her wings and dropped.

She flew gracefully through the air in this rhythmic, undulating flight.

Sunshine neared her favorite hunting spot on a street of houses directly across from a small patch of woods. She found the bugs juicy and numerous among the manicured lawns. The bugs literally jumped out of the grass here.

She landed in the nearest yard, and her thoughts immediately went back to Treetop and the three new babies.

Everything was so different this time.

She couldn't quite understand it either. After their other babies had hatched, everything had been so good. Every single egg had hatched to reveal a fragile but living baby eager to begin life.

All the other births had made her feel so happy inside.

But her happiness was tainted this time…

She stood perfectly still, and then she cocked her head to one side and peered intently at the blades of grass, searching for movement. After a few seconds had passed and no bug revealed itself, Sunshine used the oldest trick in the book.

Sunshine held her lithe body completely still with her head to one side. She spread her wings one-third fully extended and held them still for a full second. Continuing her stop-motion movements, she now spread her wings half-way and again held them in position for less than a second before fully extending them.

In the next moment, she folded her wings back against her body.

Nothing moved.

She took two quick steps forward and repeated the stop-motion action of extending her wings. This trick of mockingbirds was used to startle any bugs into movement so they could be pounced upon.

Finally, the trick worked.

As the shadow of her wings crossed a patch of grass, several small bugs jumped.

Sunshine snatched first one and then several more with rapid strikes of her sharp beak. She felt satisfaction knowing that soon her babies would have more food.

Sunshine hopped a few feet forward, stirred up some more bugs, and efficiently consumed them.

But the strange, gnawing fear struck her heart again.

She tried to analyze her turbulent emotions, but the fear inside her heart suddenly exploded. Her entire body shook for a moment. With great effort, she pushed it all away and focused on finding more bugs. It was almost like she was running on automatic pilot now: find food and feed the babies; do what needs to be done.

She had perfected this act of denial ever since she realized yesterday morning that one of the babies was deformed. She and Treetop had flung themselves into feeding the babies. In so doing, there wasn't time to think; there wasn't time to fear.

One of them would sit on the babies until the other returned with food. While that parent dropped the warm, juicy protein down one open, pleading beak after another, the other would leap into the air and hunt for bugs. As soon as they had filled their maw with the gently digested protein, they would fly back and take their mate's place. They repeated the routine over and over again.

Treetop and Sunshine threw themselves into this routine performed by all parents since the beginning of time. They did it with joy. They did it because they wanted to do it and because they had to do it. They were good parents.

But something was terribly wrong inside her heart, and it frightened her.

She went back to hunting. She couldn't deal with this dark, foreboding fear that came and went like some ominous breeze right before a storm. It felt as if the storm would explode at any moment.

She wanted to be happy so badly.

She was supposed to be happy…

Sunshine continued feeding until she realized her maw was full. She also realized that more time had passed than she intended. Treetop would be tired and probably hungry himself.

She flapped her wings and leapt into the air to return to her babies. But even though the joy of flight filled her heart as she soared above the trees, the all-too-familiar dread returned. Fear filled her heart once again -- a dark foreboding filled her being.

She flew faster!

Overwhelming panic suddenly gripped her soul, and she felt an irresistible urge to fly far away. In that instant, she realized what she feared so much -- *she was afraid to return and find the baby dead.*

Sunshine veered away from the tree that held the nest and her young and flew away as fast as her wings would carry her.

Yes, that was exactly what she feared -- that was the deep, dark, dread that killed her joy and even made her question whether life was worth living now.

She was afraid she would return and find the poor baby dead.

What would she do then?

Fear gripped her entire being. *She had to get away.*

She couldn't handle this... It was just too much. After all, how could she help this poor baby? How could she teach it to hop, much less fly?

Treetop was right: he would certainly die!

And she just couldn't face that terrible eventuality.

She didn't know how long she flew away in fear. All she knew through the fog of confusion inside her mind was that she had to fly. On and on, she flew. Her vision blurred, and the branches of a large tree appeared. She turned away and flew faster. Now a strong headwind pummeled her body and caused her to lose altitude. She turned again so the wind aided her flight. Her mind was filled with confusion – again and again she changed direction while she flew among the trees. And with each change of direction, she flew ever faster.

All at once, she broke through the maze of tree limbs and flew out into the open air.

She realized she was heading back to the nest.

But how?

Inside her heart, she knew she had to feed the babies. She had to care for them.

After all, she was the mother.

A new feeling grew inside her heart as she drew near the nest. It was a powerful feeling that fought against the terrible dread. A new determination pounded inside her heart; a new sense of purpose filled her being and pushed against the dark emptiness.

Quickly, she channeled this new surge of energy.

She felt it deep inside her heart, more deeply than she had ever felt any emotion in her entire life. It gave her such clarity of thought that she knew exactly what she had to do.

She would feed all three babies. She would nurture each and every baby. She would teach each one how to fly. Both she and her mate would raise them just as they had done with all the others.

Somehow, they would do it.

The baby with only one leg would live. And not only would it live -- it would thrive.

This newfound determination filled Sunshine's entire being with power.

And inside her mind, one thought echoed over and over again.

No baby of mine is going to die!

Chapter Three

"It's all my fault," Treetop whispered to himself.

He reached down and fed the oldest baby, who swallowed the regurgitated goo with great, appreciative gulps. But as soon as the baby got the final, juicy morsel down into its crop, he opened his mouth and pleaded for more.

"Feed me! Feed me!"

Treetop sighed with sadness.

Deep inside his heart, he blamed himself for this tragedy. He didn't know how or why, but he felt the poor baby's deformity had to be his fault. He hated himself for it.

And when the baby died, he would be the one to dispose of the body, though he didn't know if he had the strength to perform the tragic deed when the time came.

Somehow, he had to be brave for the two healthy babies and especially for Sunshine. He was trying so hard to put on a brave face, trying to act like everything was normal.

But everything wasn't normal.

And he didn't really feel brave, no matter how hard he tried.

"Feed me! Feed me!"

The other two babies, nodding with sleep while their brother had taken his turn, now came alive and raised their heads with mouths opened wide.

Three open mouths beckoned up at him.

25

Treetop paused a moment and smiled.

He watched the smallest baby, the baby with one leg, try to rise and get his mouth above his siblings and receive his share. Treetop's heart pounded rapidly while he focused on the youngest one. Unlike his siblings, the little guy could not balance. His head swayed unsteadily as he tried to push his body up with his one leg.

With a burst of energy, the one-legged baby lifted himself above the others, and he cried out eagerly.

Treetop's heart dropped when the baby fell back and rolled on its left side -- the side with the missing leg. The little fellow struggled to right himself while the other two easily raised themselves higher on their wobbly legs and asked for more.

The two healthy babies held themselves up -- for a brief moment. But their still weak legs and untrained sense of balance caused each to fall back down in quick succession as well.

Still, they sat down. They didn't fall over helplessly like the poor one-legged baby.

He wanted to cry, but he couldn't -- not in front of the babies. And certainly not in front of Sunshine.

He had to be strong, even if it was simply an appearance and inside he was uncertain and afraid. He was the head of the family, and the father, well, the father was always strong, it was his role.

He also had to do it for the other birds too. They expected it, it was normal. He had to prove to everyone that he was strong and that his family was just like any … that his family was…

Treetop groaned.

He didn't want others thinking he was a failure, that he was a bad father, and that's exactly what he feared they would think of him when they discovered he had a deformed baby. And more so, when it died.

He sighed bitterly. He would think he was failure.

But deep inside, it bothered him even more what others would think of him.

***

With a fluttering of feathers, Sunshine flew through the branches and landed on the branch opposite the nest from him. She smiled at him and glanced lovingly at their babies. He saw she had been successful and was ready to take her turn feeding the babies.

She glanced at him with her eyes glowing.

"We mustn't get too attached to him." Treetop looked away from her startled expression.

"What!" Sunshine shouted angrily. She hopped right next to him and stared into his yellow eyes. "Have you already given up? You… you just expect that baby to die!"

Treetop hopped up and down excitedly, shocked at her outburst. He looked nervously over at the babies, who stared in silent shock at them.

"Shhhhh," Treetop urged. "They can hear us."

"Don't you 'shhh' me!" She glared at him. but

then lowered her voice to a whisper. "We're the parents. Shouldn't we do everything in our power help him?"

"Yes... yes we should. But I'm just trying to be practical..." he whispered back.

"I don't want to be practical. I am determined to keep this baby alive!" Sunshine twittered rapidly. "We are going raise all these babies. All of them, every single baby, will learn to fly. All of them will leave the nest."

She pressed her beak right up against the side of his head and whispered her next words fiercely.

"Yes, even that baby with only one leg is going to live. I vowed to myself just now that I won't let him die. Not now, not ever."

She stared with angry determination at him.

Treetop didn't know what to say. He didn't know how to explain his feelings. He didn't know what to do.

"I don't know."

"I don't want to talk to you anymore." She turned her back on him.

Treetop let out a sigh. He hopped up beside her. They were perched side by side on a branch much as they had done most of their adult lives. He looked down at his own three-toed feet and spoke again.

"I'm just... well, I'm just trying to think it through." He paused as he gathered his troubled thoughts. "How can the little bird ever learn to stand? In a few days, the babies will double in size. The nest will be crowded. The babies will begin to push each other as they test out their wings and their newly grown feathers. And... and they'll begin to move around the nest. And..."

A look of growing concern spread over Sunshine's face.

"And what?" she prompted.

"The little guy will get pushed around. He won't get his fair share of food as the other two stand above him. They'll crowd him out more and more until... *until they push him out of the nest.*"

Treetop looked away as Sunshine caught her breath quickly, almost as if she were about to break down and cry.

His heart sank deeper and deeper into a well of anguish.

"How can the poor guy compete for food, for space, with his two healthy siblings?" Treetop's tone had an edge of somber finality.

"We'll make sure he gets enough to eat!" Sunshine shot back. "If the other two push him out of the way, we'll push them aside. And if we have to we will force the food down his open beak. We'll help him."

A strange expression crossed Treetop's countenance.

"It's the way of things, Sunshine. The strong survive. The weak die," he said simply.

"No! I won't accept that! Absolutely not!" Sunshine hopped up to the next higher branch with a sudden burst of energy. She glared down at Treetop and began speaking in rapid-fire staccato. "We've got to give him a chance. If he lives long enough to fly the nest, I think he can survive. After all, he has two wings! He has a beak! He just needs to learn how to stand and hop on one leg!"

"I'll feed him as long as he is able to get his beak up along with the others. But if they push him away…" His unuttered words spoke volumes.

Sunshine spread her wings and hopped back down beside Treetop.

"Listen, he needs a break. We can give him a start. Maybe he can learn to stand on one leg. If we can just keep him strong until his feathers grow and he's ready to fly." Sunshine's eyes pleaded to Treetop.

Treetop sighed deeply.

"I'll make sure he gets as much as the others. And maybe a little more," Sunshine said with determination. "You just do your part and feed 'each' baby when it's your turn."

"If they push him aside…" Treetop began.

Sunshine hopped right into his face, her breath hot against his face.

"If I find you neglecting that one-legged baby, I'm going to peck you on the head so hard you won't be able to fly straight for a week!"

A shocked expression passed over Treetop's face. He looked at his mate thoughtfully.

"Okay, I'll try. But…." Treetop's plaintive expression turned serious. "We can't fight nature."

"Yes, we can! Even if I have to neglect my share of the food and give it to him, I'm going to make sure he has his chance. I just want to see him get his feathers and fly the nest. I want it more than anything I've ever wanted my entire life."

The two mockingbirds stood in silence a long moment.

The green leaves of the dogwood slowly began to dance and flutter as a summer breeze swept the air. Hundreds of leaves danced as though choreographed by the invisible force of the wind, and the subtle rustling filled the air with a soft, mesmerizing sound.

The whole world was movement around them, but the two birds stood oblivious to the beauty surrounding them.

As the wind picked up, leaves on the slender stalks waved in faster, circular motions while larger branches began gently swaying. Even the nest built solidly into the fork of a large branch moved up and down and slightly sideways under the power of the wind.

Treetop's mind raced. His mate's words echoed over and over in his mind. And as he stood there, it seemed somehow that some of Sunshine's newfound resolution seeped into his heart.

Gradually, almost imperceptibly, the wind faded. The dancing leaves slowed their circular movements, and the larger branches grew still, signaling the end of the wind dance.

"Tomorrow, their down will be thicker and they'll be able to keep themselves warm. We can both fly away together and get food and bring it back. We'll double their feedings that way," Treetop said with newfound confidence.

"Yes! That's the spirit!" Sunshine chirped

happily.

Somehow, his mate's determination inspired him. The more he thought about it, the more he felt her idea might work.

"Let's feed these babies so much that they won't have time to peep -- *'feed me! feed me!'*" Treetop chuckled, and Sunshine laughed out loud along with him.

He kissed her tenderly. "You feed them while I go find more food." Treetop took wing.

While he hunted and snatched bug after bug, he felt better. He knew how to feed babies. He knew how to take care of them. And most of all, he knew how to hunt bugs.

When he returned and landed beside her with a full gullet, Sunshine's eyes sparkled with delight. She whistled a brief and happy melody and quickly flew off to get more food.

Treetop fed each baby in quick succession. As soon as he filled the mouth of one baby, he turned to another, round and round, until they each settled down into the nest in silent concentration while their full bellies digested the food.

He waited a moment, watching all three carefully. He knew Sunshine would be away for several more minutes. He wanted to try something, but he didn't know if it would work, and he didn't want to try it when she was around -- just in case.

"Baby, um, baby. I want you to watch Daddy closely."

Three sets of eyes opened.

"No, just you, over there." Treetop nodded

toward the smallest.

Three sets of eyes watched him intently.

"Okay, well, all of you can watch." He cleared his throat nervously. "But I want you to watch closely -- and learn. All right?"

The one-legged baby opened his beak in a smile and nodded.

The other two smiled and nodded too.

"Good." Treetop hopped a little closer to the nest. "Watch closely."

He squatted down until his legs disappeared under his body.

"Now, I'm going to lift myself up because I'm hungry, and I want Daddy to feed me."

Three tiny voices laughed with pleasure.

"No, no, pretend with me now. I'm a baby, just like you three. And I'm hungry and want more." He waited until their laughter subsided.

"Now, watch me -- watch my leg -- closely."

Slowly, he lifted his body up from the branch using only one leg. He swayed unsteadily a moment and then fell down on his rump with a rush of feathers.

"Funny Daddy! Funny Daddy!" They all giggled with glee.

Treetop felt a little embarrassed -- at first -- but the laughter of the babies made him feel happy inside. He laughed with them a moment, his mirth mingling with theirs.

After the happy sounds subsided, the three babies continued to watch him intently, waiting for the next round of entertainment.

But now he realized just how hard a thing it was to try and stand on only one leg. He had tried and lost his own balance, and somehow he expected a newly hatched baby to learn this?

"Do it again, Daddy!" the babies chirped excitedly.

"Hang on."

He closed his eyes and concentrated.

The babies watched expectantly with their beaks open in bird-smiles.

After a long moment, he tried again.

He felt all three babies stare with unblinking intensity at him.

Slowly, methodically, he lifted himself up using just one leg. He felt himself begin to sway unsteadily when he got about halfway up. This time, however, instead of falling back down, he spread his wings in order to maintain his balance.

Treetop felt both his balance and his confidence return. His heart thumped with excitement as he held himself in that position, wings partially extended and standing on one leg with the other leg bent under his body.

"See how I used my wings to balance myself so I didn't fall down. Now, I'll lift myself up all the way."

Slowly, he straightened his leg until he stood completely up. Treetop watched them observe him closely as he stood before them on one leg.

He held his pose a long time, willing the smallest baby to comprehend the lesson he was trying to teach.

The smallest baby smiled at him happily.

Suddenly, he heard the familiar sound of wings drawing close.

He dropped his second leg down and stood on both legs just as Sunshine landed.

The three babies laughed with delight.

"Do it again, Daddy! Play the game again!" they shouted together.

Sunshine looked at him with a puzzled expression. "What game were you playing?"

"Ah, nothing -- nothing. It was just a... a game."

"Play it again!" they shouted again.

Treetop felt embarrassment warming his face. "Get your dinner from Mom here. If you're all good babies, I'll play it again later."

At the mention of food, their cries changed to the all-too-familiar chorus. "Feed me! Feed me!"

"I'll go find some more bugs." Treetop quickly launched himself into the wind.

When he looked back over his shoulder, Sunshine was smiling back at him.

Chapter Four

He's not getting enough to eat.

That single, frightening fact permeated their existence. Unspoken between them, a terrible fear darkened their hearts as the one-legged baby struggled to get his share of food. The fear was so powerful it haunted all their waking moments and colored their every emotion.

Sunshine and Treetop couldn't put words to the terrible, consuming emotion -- almost as if giving voice to the fear might make it come true.

But when they looked into each other's eyes, they recognized their own fear.

Two days passed in frenzied activity.

Treetop demonstrated again and again to the one-legged baby how to raise himself up on one leg. Treetop quickly mastered the action as he used his wings less and less for balance.

But although the tiny baby watched intently, he never lifted himself up even once, and now he was half the size of his healthy siblings.

His brother and sister were easily raising themselves above him on their two legs and getting most of the food while he struggled awkwardly. At every feeding, the healthy siblings pushed and positioned themselves over him while he cried and pleaded for food.

Treetop and Sunshine both tried to focus their attention on him, but one of the other healthy babies usually pushed him aside and took his portion.

Treetop's heart beat sadly as he crouched low on the branch. The one-legged baby sat with closed eyes. He slept so much now, conserving his strength as he grew continually weaker.

"Are you watching me, little one?" Treetop asked with a hush.

"Yes, Daddy!" the little girl peeped excitedly.

"Me too," shouted the eldest male, raising himself up on two legs.

Treetop looked at the third baby, who crouched forlornly in the nest.

The one-legged baby opened his eyes.

Huddled in one corner of the nest, his body wobbled as he pushed with his one leg. He knew what to try now. But as he stretched his leg to lift himself, he always pushed himself over instead of upward. He tried in vain to use his small, down-covered wings to gain his balance.

In sharp contrast, his two siblings sat straight and still and perfectly balanced, their heads cocked to the side with their attention focused on him. As their smaller brother struggled anew, they looked over at him with puzzled expressions.

Treetop didn't know what to do.

It was happening exactly as he'd feared. The one-legged baby was not getting his share of food. And worse, his endless struggles to raise himself up were draining his energy. It seemed the little baby was getting weaker and weaker with each passing day.

Treetop's heart sank with despair.

"Well, well, Treetop. I'd heard you and

37

Sunshine had a new brood. Why haven't you sent word?"

Treetop looked up to find Aunt Coldrain perched on a branch above him. He cringed involuntarily.

"Oh, hello, Aunty. I don't know ... we've just been too busy."

Coldrain hopped down beside him. "Let me get a closer look at the babies," she chirped brusquely.

His anguish deepened as she gazed from one baby to the other.

At just that moment, Sunshine returned.

"How many males?" Coldrain asked.

"Two. And one female. She hatched between them," Sunshine replied emotionlessly, glancing pensively from the babies to Coldrain.

Coldrain turned to her with a disconcerting gaze. "You don't sound very happy, Sunshine?"

Sunshine sighed. "I'm just… tired."

"Ah yes, feeding three healthy babies will do that every time." Coldrain laughed.

Treetop closed his eyes and groaned at her words -- 'three *healthy* babies.'

Coldrain returned to her examination of the babies. Both Treetop and Sunshine felt their hearts freeze as her piercing gaze fell upon the littlest baby sitting awkwardly in the corner of the nest.

"What's the matter with that baby?"

"Uh, he's just smaller than the others," Treetop replied.

Coldrain hopped closer and peered intently at him. "He is awfully small. Aren't you feeding him?"

"Of course we're feeding him!" Sunshine replied sharply.

Aunty looked at Sunshine with an odd expression. "No need to get upset, deary, but he's almost half the size of his brother and sister. One can't help but notice how tiny and frail he is. Poor, poor baby."

Treetop quickly hopped next to Sunshine. "She's just an old bird, honey," he whispered hurriedly before Sunshine's anger erupted again. "She doesn't mean to say things, so harshly. She's-
_"

"Hush, Treetop!" Sunshine snapped. She turned to Aunt Coldrain. "You don't have to be so critical, Aunty. We're doing the best we can. Some babies just don't grow as fast as others. You should know that!"

"Hmmmph." Coldrain fluffed her feathers with irritation. "What I meant is -- why is he sitting in such an odd position? Is there something underneath him causing him to lean over like that?"

"He's all right," Treetop said quickly. "And, really, we need to feed all of them again. If you don't mind, we'd like to do that now."

Treetop approached the nest in preparation for another feeding.

But Coldrain wouldn't go away.

"The 'Naming Day' must be near, right? At least, the two larger babies look to be around five days old now." She looked closely at the littlest baby again. "Although it's hard to tell with him."

Sunshine and Treetop looked at each other in surprise.

In their constant care and feeding, all of it overshadowed by their fear and sadness, they had completely forgotten what day it was.

Coldrain was correct -- the babies were five days old now.

It was the way of all birds. On the seventh day, right after the sun rose above the trees and into the sky, all relatives gathered near the nest for the 'Naming Day.' At that important milestone in a baby bird's life, the parents named each baby before the on-lookers in preparation for the babies' final week in the nest.

After that, they would hop onto the nearest branches and begin a new phase of life. And very soon after that important day, they would learn to fly.

"Yes." Sunshine paused, as if afraid. She took a deep breath and continued. "Yes, they are five days old."

"Good!" Coldrain hopped excitedly. "I'll fly around to the relatives and let them all know! We'll all gather here in this tree and share your joy as you name each darling baby."

With a flash of feathers, she flew away.

Sunshine sighed with exasperation.

Treetop closed his eyes while his heart pounded. He opened them a long moment later and discovered Sunshine gone. He looked around hurriedly until he finally spotted her high in the top of the tree. He flew up and perched near her on the topmost branch, but she kept her back to him in silence.

He felt a new wave of sadness when he realized she was crying.

"It's all right, Sunshine. Aunty Coldrain is an old, crotchety bird. Her words are harsher than she intends."

Sunshine's shoulders shuddered with her sobs.

"There, there. Just do what I do when she talks," Treetop said comfortingly.

She looked at him with tears in her eyes. "What?"

"Ignore her."

Sunshine choked back her laughter.

"Well, I ignore most of what she says."

She smiled at him, but then she quickly hung her head down and stared at her feet. "I'm a failure."

Her words cut Treetop's heart like a knife.

"No, you're not," he replied quickly and firmly.

"Yes. Yes, I am. I'm a failure as a mother."

Treetop cringed. "Why? Why do you feel that way? We've raised so many babies together already! They've all left the nest and added their voices to the 'Song of Life.'"

"I don't want this baby to die, but he gets smaller and smaller no matter how much I feed him. Nothing I do helps. I -- I can't do anything right..." Her tears streamed down her face.

Treetop hopped beside Sunshine and put his wings around her. "We can do more. We won't let him die."

"H-h-how?" She sobbed.

He thought a moment, his mind burning with activity as he tried to think of something, anything, they might try. Suddenly, an idea materialized.

"We'll feed them together."

A puzzled expression crossed her face. "How will that help?"

"The two babies are stronger and getting more than he is. I'll feed them from one side of the nest while you feed the one-legged baby from the other side!"

Sunshine's eyes widened with hope. "That could work."

Treetop felt a surge of joy in his heart. "It will work. It will mean we can't rotate, one after the other taking turns feeding them. It'll be harder on us, both of us hunting simultaneously and feeding them simultaneously."

"It will be hard, but it will be worth it if he grows stronger," she replied enthusiastically.

Treetop smiled at her. He felt so good inside and really felt his idea might work. The anguish and fear tried to return, but he fought them. And deep, deep inside he felt a yearning, a powerful longing, to have a 'normal family' once again, though nothing seemed normal anymore.

"Should we start now?" Sunshine asked hesitantly.

Treetop shook his thoughts aside. "Yes. Let me go hunt right now. I know you just returned ready to feed them, but wait until I return. I'll be back as quick as I can!"

With a flash of gray feathers, he flew away.

Treetop flew as fast as he could fly, soaring through the summer breeze while eying the houses on the street below him. Earlier, he had smelled the wonderfully familiar fragrance of grass being cut, and he soon spotted the freshly mown lawn. He dove with a flash of the white spots on his wings.

In quick fashion, he hunted up and down the lawn until he'd gorged himself on the juicy bugs that seemed to be everywhere today. With his craw full, he soared on the wind back to the nest.

Sunshine was perched beside the babies waiting expectantly for him. He smiled at her as he landed next to the two healthy babies.

"Okay, I'll feed these two, and you feed the little one!"

Treetop bent over, opened his mouth, and fed first one and then the other. As soon as both got a large mouthful and sat down digesting the first morsel, he glanced over at Sunshine. She carefully fed the little one with small but steady morsels, Treetop smiled with an inner warmth of satisfaction.

"Feed me! Feed me!" chirped the two healthy babies.

He smiled down at them and again fed them.

All the rest of that day, Sunshine and Treetop diligently fed all three babies simultaneously. On the following day, the sixth, they again rose with the sun as the morning chorus of the birds echoed in the air, but they were too busy to add their voices and welcome another day of life.

All through the long hours, they flew and hunted

and returned with food for all three babies. Over and over again, they fed the babies until their eyes fluttered and they all fell asleep with full bellies. In those all-too-brief moments, Sunshine and Treetop would try to get a little food for themselves.

More importantly, after they had grabbed a quick bite, they perched together close to the nest and got as much rest as possible before the babies awoke hungry again.

The three babies slept now, contented with full bellies.

Treetop and Sunshine settled down for a quick nap themselves.

Treetop's eyes slowly closed. Through half-closed eyelids, his gaze traveled from one baby to the other until he stopped on the little one-legged baby. Their feathers were now rapidly replacing their newborn coating of down. In fact, they were beginning to finally resemble baby mockingbirds.

He watched that one baby, surveying the new feathers that covered his back. There was something else... his tired mind told him. Or was it just wishful thinking?

As his eyelids started to close all the way, he suddenly jerked wide awake, refocusing on the littlest baby. For in that instant before his eyes had shut completely, it seemed the one-legged baby had lifted itself up and stood on its one leg.

But as he watched now, the baby simply sat resting in the nest.

As he stared, his heart pounding rapidly under his breast, he wondered: Had he dreamed it? Or had

Bluesky and Sunshine

the baby really stood up for a brief moment?

Chapter Five

The house located at 3477 Willow Hollow was a typical two-story frame structure. The Wentworth family had it painted three years ago right after they moved in. It now sported a creamy yellow gloss over its sides, accented with ocean green trim on the shutters and doors. Green and black shingles had been installed on the roof even more recently and added to the newfound luster of the fifteen-year-old dwelling.

Mark Wentworth walked out the back door onto the concrete patio and pulled the cover off the grill in preparation for the cookout. He hummed a melody by Mozart as he picked up the cooking rack and brought it inside the kitchen for a good cleaning. While he ran the hot, soapy water over it, he paid extra attention so as not to mess up the kitchen too much. His wife would soon be cooking the side dishes and making the summer salad here to accompany the hamburger and hot dogs he would be grilling.

He smiled at the sound of footsteps as his four-year-old son came running down the stairs, his seven-year-old daughter in hot pursuit.

"Kate, don't chase your brother down the stairs. How many times have I warned you two about that!" Mark didn't even turn his head at the sound of the two panting in the doorway behind him.

"But, Daddy, he pulled my hair," Kate protested plaintively.

"It's not true, Dad!" Philip countered immediately. "I mean, I didn't mean to do it."

"See, Daddy!" Kate added. "He did it, and he meant to!"

"Enough, you two." Mark turned and smiled at them as he stood in front of the sink. "Kate, did you get the card table out like your mother asked?"

Her bright blue eyes gleamed. "Yes, it's in the rec room already."

Mark's gaze rested on young Philip. "Young man, did you pick up your toys like you were asked?"

Philip's mischievous smile grew even bigger. "Yep, done done it. I'm ready to play with Scott!"

The Harrells were coming over, along with two other couples, but the kids were most excited about seeing the Harrell family since they alone had children. Mandy was six, Scott was five, and their baby not quite one year old.

"Can we play when they get here?" Philip pleaded.

"Sure. You can play outside while I grill. After we eat, we'll play some games inside," Mark replied. He walked toward the back door with the freshly cleaned rack. "Go get the Frisbee and our gloves and a baseball. We'll play a little now."

"Great!" Kate and Philip shouted together. They ran into the rec room and promptly emerged with the items in hand.

Mark put the rack in place and then turned on the gas and lit the flame. He turned and took the Frisbee from Kate.

"Everybody likes coming to our house to grill out," Kate said gleefully.

"Oh, why is that?" Mark asked his daughter.

"Cause we have birds and butterflies," Philip chimed in.

"And hummingbirds too," Kate added quickly.

Mark smiled.

"Why do we have so many?" Kate asked with a puzzled expression.

"Well, we have a small stand of woods to the side and behind our house. And a small creek runs through the woods too. But the main reason we have birds and butterflies is because I plant bushes and trees that attract them."

"And you feed them!" Kate cried out joyfully.

"And you feed your enemies too!" Philip laughed hysterically.

Mark grunted to himself at the mention of his furry archenemies. "Yes, we have two bird feeders, and I keep them filled up. And I do my best to keep the squirrels away."

"And hummingbirds, dad! I like them the best!" Philip shouted with glee.

"Yes, we have a hummingbird feeder, too. And I've planted holly bushes and lantana and a few other plants that birds and butterflies love."

The two children ran halfway across the fenced-in backyard and now waited expectantly for their dad to throw the Frisbee.

Mark smiled at their youthful exuberance as he tossed the Frisbee toward his daughter. Of course, Philip ran over and tried to intercept, but his older sister easily reached over him and snatched the flying saucer out of his grasp.

"Dad!" Philip complained loudly. "I wanted to catch it!"

"I'll throw the next one to you."

Kate gloated over her little brother a moment and then threw it back to her dad with a practiced flip of her wrist.

"Good throw, Katie!"

"Dad, why don't other people have birds like we do?"

"Well, some people cut down all the trees around their house. The birds have no place to build their nests or roost at night. And birds like bushes too. If people don't have bushes, they won't have birds either."

"Honey!" Jane shouted sweetly from the opened back door. "Did you clean the grill? Folks will start arriving anytime."

"Yes, Jane. Everything's ready. All I have to do is put the meat on."

His wife smiled first at him and then over to their children, who now ran around each other in an impromptu game of tag.

Jane was a pretty woman with light brown hair and brown eyes and a medium build. Her face and eyes still reflected youthful freshness and vitality.

"Okay, the salad is ready, and I'll go ahead and put on the baked beans and start boiling the corn on the cob." She disappeared back inside the house.

"Philip, get ready." Mark slowly brought his arm around in preparation of his throw, and then with a quick motion he tossed the disc to his son.

The Frisbee sailed right into the outstretched hands of Philip, but it bounced away before the boy could close his fingers around the disc.

The little boy immediately covered his face with both hands and sat down on the ground with a comically exaggerated gesture of sadness. The little boy became the perfect picture of utter and total dejection.

Mark repressed an urge to laugh. He realized his son was distraught in spite of his childishly embellished expressions of frustration.

"Hey, son, you almost had it. You just need to keep your eyes on it all the way into your hands."

"Oh, Dad! I'll never be able to catch it!" His eyes moistened with tears as he uttered a sigh of resignation.

"Now, now. You'll get better." Mark walked over and sat down in the grass beside his son.

Katie ran over and sat down on the other side of Philip. Tenderly, she put her arm around her little brother's shoulders.

"You'll learn, Philip," Katie said. "I had trouble when I was little like you, but you'll get the hang of it."

Mark smiled at his daughter's sincere concern. He looked back down at the sad frown on Philip's face.

"Every time we play together, you'll get a little better, son," Mark said with a reassuring tone. "Don't give up. If you give up, you'll never learn. Keep trying. Just like Katie said, you might miss a few at first, but you'll learn, and then it will get easier and more fun."

Philip, energized by all the concern around him, jumped up, ran toward the fence, and turned with his hands open and ready. He smiled at his dad as he waited for the Frisbee.

Mark walked closer to his son until they were only ten feet apart.

"Catch it, son."

He tossed it as gently as he could toward Philip's outstretched hands.

Philip caught it easily.

"Good. Toss it back and let's do it again."

Philip tossed it end-over-end at his dad, and the Frisbee landed nowhere close to Mark.

Mark picked it up and again gently tossed it back to his son.

Philip caught it again.

After every successful catch by Philip, Mark would walk backward and increase the distance between them. Now, he had to toss the Frisbee with more spin so it could cross the entire distance. He patiently repeated the tosses until Philip was able to catch it almost every time.

Mark saw Philip's confidence growing with each catch.

"Remember, Philip, it's spinning. When you grab it, hang on even though it's spinning."

The Frisbee bounce off Phillip's hands a few times as he was still not used to the faster spin of the flying object, but he was able to hang on and catch it more and more.

Mark tossed it a little harder and with a faster spin, and Philip caught it and held on tightly.

"Good job!"

Mark now walked away until almost twenty feet separated them. It was time for the real test.

"Okay, keep your eyes on it the whole way."

"I'm ready, Dad!"

"You can do it!" Katie cheered.

Mark extended his arm and aimed the Frisbee at his son. With a smooth flick of his wrist, he sent the Frisbee on a steady and level flight straight to the hands of his waiting son.

Philip cried out gleefully as the Frisbee sailed through the air right at him, and with a shout of sheer joy, the little boy snatched the Frisbee and held on tight.

"I did it! I did it, Dad!"

"Good job, Philip. Yes, you really caught it!"

"Hooray, Philip!" Katie jumped up and down as all of them shared Philip's happiness.

Mark turned toward a knocking sound. He smiled when he saw Jane peering out at him and the children through the kitchen window, her hand still at the pane where she had just knocked. Mark realized she must have watched the entire scene play out -- her husband playing with the children in their backyard.

He smiled at her, and she smiled back.

"Hi, Mommy!" Philip and Katie shouted together.

Jane signaled her pleasure at Philip's achievement by giving him a 'thumbs up.'

Philip and Katie clapped with joy when Mark caught sight of a gray bird with a bright white patch on its wings flying overhead.

"Did you two see that?"

Philip and Kate looked up, but the mockingbird was already out of sight as it flew over the roof of the house.

"Did you know that bird has a nest in our dogwood tree over there?" Mark asked his children.

"Really? Can we see the baby birds, Dad? Kate pleaded as she and Philip ran up to him.

"I've noticed the mother and father bird going back and forth feeding their babies the last few days when I sit at the window in the breakfast nook."

Mark took each child by the hand and walked over to the trunk of the old dogwood tree. The three of them peered upward through the leaf-laden branches. After a moment, Mark spotted the small nest in the fork of a branch about halfway up.

"There, see where that branch forks." Mark squatted down until his head was level with his children and pointed up toward the nest.

"Yes! I see it!" Katie whispered excitedly.

"I don't see it!" Philip whined.

Mark put his right arm around his son and now pointed with his left hand.

"Oh, I see it! Are there baby birds in it?"

"Yes, listen quietly a moment." Mark raised his forefinger to his lips.

A light breeze caused the leaves in the tree to rustle and flutter all above them. The three of them gazed in silence, waiting for a sound to indicate there were baby birds in the nest.

Suddenly, a mature mockingbird appeared out of nowhere and landed on a branch across from the nest. The bird cocked its head and looked straight down at the three humans.

"Be still," Mark urged as he felt his son and daughter start to squirm.

Suddenly a sound came to their ears -- the diminutive and eager cries of baby birds begging to be fed.

Kate and Philip turned with wide eyes to their father.

He smiled at them. "See, there are baby birds in the nest, and they want to be fed. Let's leave the momma bird alone so she can feed them." He took them both by the hand and led them toward the patio.

"Can we see the baby birds?" Kate asked.

"We'll see them when they learn to fly. Mom and Dad will keep their babies close by for a while, until the babies get good at flying. We'll see them flying around the yard."

"That'll be great," Philip said excitedly. "I wish I was a bird so I could learn to fly!"

"Me too," Mark added with sincerity. "It must be a wonderful thing to have wings and fly up into the wide-open sky."

***

Our Feathered Friends of the Southeast
A. C. Wages

Northern Mockingbird
Latin: *Mimus polyglottos*   (English: many-tongued mimic)

(excerpt)

A familiar bird throughout the Southeastern United States, its range extends into the Midwest and Western states and up through most of the Northern states now. The mockingbird is also found in many islands of the Caribbean. This fabulous songster is equally at home in the yards of suburbia as well as the inner cities. It is also found on the coasts and in the forests, as well as fields and dales.

A medium-sized songbird, the Northern Mockingbird has pale gray feathers on its head and back with whitish feathers below. Their wings are gray-black with two white wing bars. However, when they spread their wings a 'white patch' is clearly visible at mid-wing, reminding one of an insignia on the wing of a fighter plane.

Males and females are identical in coloration.

Their long, graceful tails are edged with white feathers while the central feathers are gray-black. Their piercing eyes range in color from pale yellow to orange.

The mockingbird is fiercely territorial

(fiercely loyal). This powerful tendency is amplified while protecting a nest with eggs. In fact, mockingbirds have been known to dive-bomb cats, snakes, and even people passing too close to the nest if they perceive them as a threat. Even more bizarre, some mockingbirds have targeted specific individuals who frequent the area near their nest and will dive-bomb them alone while they ignore other people passing along the same way!

A mockingbird adds to its repertoire of songs all the days of its life.

Many famous observations have been made of this bird and its extraordinary ability to mimic the songs of any other bird it chances to hear. In addition to imitating the songs of other birds, the mockingbird is able to mimic such sounds as the hinges of a closing door, notes played by a piano, or even a snippet of a tune from a radio. The mockingbird's imitation of these sounds is so exact that in many scientific studies, electronic analysis could not distinguish the difference between the mockingbird and the real thing!

The mockingbird is the official state bird of five states: Arkansas, Florida, Mississippi, Tennessee, and Texas.

Here are two quotes describing this remarkable bird.

"The Indians, by way of eminence or

admiration, call it Cencontlatolly, or four hundred tongues; and we call it Mock-Bird, from its wonderful mocking and imitating the notes of all Birds, from the Humming Bird to the Eagle." (Mark Catesby)

"The Lark and the Nightingale in one." (Naturalist John Burroughs)

When the mockingbird was first discovered in the Americas and brought back to Europe, people marveled at how easily and exactly it mimicked even the song of the nightingale!

The mockingbird is featured in the traditional American lullaby "Hush Little Baby." In one line, the lyrics read *'Mama's going to buy you a mockingbird'*, which references the fact that mockingbirds were once popular pets in America.

In the landmark novel *To Kill a Mockingbird* by Harper Lee, this bird is used as a metaphor representing innocence in this tragic tale of racial prejudice. It is brought out that mockingbirds are good birds and do no harm to anyone or anything, and thus *it is a sin to kill a mockingbird.* The metaphor poignantly applies to Tom Robinson, a humble black man accused of raping a white woman in the rural south during the time of segregation. Although innocent, he is convicted and killed by the majority white population because of their blind prejudice.

A Cherokee myth explains how all birds

first got their songs and humorously explains why the mockingbird can imitate the song of every other bird. In the myth, the only bird who can sing is the mockingbird. The mockingbird sings countless songs all day and all night to the delight of all the other animals. All the other birds eventually come to the mockingbird and ask him for a song of their own so they can sing like him. He bestows on each bird their own individual song by singing it to them until they learn to sing it themselves. And to this day, each family of birds sings its own unique song -- but the mockingbird can sing them all!

The mockingbird is a matchless minstrel, often rising early and seeking out the highest branch or perch from where it will sing for the entire world to hear. Unlike other birds, the 'mocker' will sing morning, noon, and even through the night if the mood for song strikes. In fact, some mockingbirds have been known to sing continuously all day and all night, especially lonely males earnestly seeking a mate. This bird's songs are so persistent and so powerful that one can easily recognize the songster as a mockingbird long before they see him perched high above, giving voice to his heart and soul.

Chapter Six

Sunshine had just flown up to the nest with a nice fat worm for her babies when she noticed the intruders down below. She saw the three humans, a parent with two of its young, pointing up at her. For a moment, she felt they might be after her babies, especially now that her little ones were crying out excitedly on hearing her arrival, but then the three humans began moving away from the tree while she gazed with protective determination down at them.

"Feed me! Feed me!" all three babies shouted together.

She placed the wiggling worm down on the branch and held it with one foot. She had to wait for Treetop so he could feed the other two while she fed the little baby. Already, he had gained weight from this new arrangement. She also felt he looked stronger and healthier, although he was still noticeably smaller than his siblings.

With her beak opened in a smile, she cocked her head to one side and gazed down at the nest and its precious occupants.

The oldest boy and girl raised themselves up on their legs with beaks wide open, begging for food, but her glance rested on the smallest baby, who struggled and fell back with each effort to raise himself up like his siblings.

Sunshine's heart sank.

"Stand up, little baby. You can do it," she said

with gentle encouragement. The one-legged bird renewed his efforts to lift himself up, but once again, the baby lost his balance. He fell over onto his sister, who pecked him, which made him quickly wiggle away.

She knew Treetop had been trying to teach the poor baby how to stand. Several times in the last couple of days she had flown to the tree and discovered him standing on one leg right before the baby. Sunshine had watched in silence, her heart pounding with love as she watched Treetop demonstrating over and over how to rise up on one leg for the baby.

But his diligent efforts seemed to be for naught.

A terrible panic gripped her heart. She closed her eyes, fighting back the terror, the cold realization that maybe nothing would help this poor baby.

"Mama, feed me!"

Sunshine opened her eyes. The little one-legged baby looked up at her from the bottom of the nest.

She hopped closer, forgetting all about the worm that fell to the ground far, far below. "Baby, listen to your mother."

All three babies grew silent as their mama stood directly over the nest, but her eyes and words were focused on the littlest baby.

"Look at those beautiful feathers on your wings now, just like your siblings."

All three babies gazed proudly at their wing feathers.

Sunshine fixed her gaze on the little baby's eyes

until his eyes focused solely on her. "Do you want to fly, baby?"

"Yes, Mama! I want to fly," the one-legged baby cried joyfully.

"You have to learn how to lift yourself up on one leg before you can learn to fly."

The baby's expression grew thoughtful as he struggled in vain to stand.

The panic rose in her heart again, but she fought it back. Still, there was a sense of renewed urgency in her voice. "Do you want to know what it's like to fly?" she asked him.

"Yes, Mama." He looked up with an eager expression.

Sunshine took a deep breath and closed her eyes. She thought back to the first time she flew into the sky.

She remembered it clearly.

Yes, every time Sunshine flew she felt some of the same thrill she had experienced that first time. It was always there each time she leapt into the air. As the air brushed across her face and her wings propelled her body through the sky and around the trees and even between the branches of trees -- she felt that same heart-pounding exhilaration.

"What's it like, Mama? I want to fly more than anything! Please, tell me!" the littlest baby begged.

"It's wonderful," Sunshine began. "It's like, it's like freedom -- freeing yourself from the ground and flying away toward the endless sky! You seem to become part of the sky. And everywhere you look, the world stretches far away and beckons you to fly that way… and over that way…" She laughed happily.

Her three babies listened intently with opened beaks.

She spread her wings wide over the nest as the babies stared at her in awe.

"It's the most exhilarating feeling. You feel the wind rushing over your feathers as you soar on the invisible currents of air! And as you fly higher, the ground and trees become smaller and smaller until you feel as if you're on top of the world." She smiled widely. "It's like a completely different world, flying high up in the sky."

"Wow!" three voices said together.

She paused, her eyes glowing with an inner fire as she tried to put into words what she felt when she took wing.

"It's absolutely breathtaking sometimes, flying way up in the sky and gazing down at the world far below. Flying is a special privilege that few creatures know and experience. And of all creatures who fly, only birds have feathers, the unique gift of our kind."

Sunshine looked from one baby to the other a moment, gazing deeply into their eyes. "And each of you will know the joy of flight."

Sunshine now fixed her gaze on the one-legged baby.

"You can know that joy, little one. You have two wings. You too will spread your wings and fly into the wide, open sky."

"Can I fly up to the clouds and touch them?"

the one-legged baby asked excitedly.

Sunshine smiled. "Yes, you will. At times the clouds are low in the sky -- white and puffy. That is the best time." She leaned close to her baby until her warm breath brushed the feathers of his head ever so slightly. "One day soon, you will touch the clouds."

"I want to fly, Mama. I really want to fly!"

"You have to stand before you can fly, little baby."

The one-legged baby became a blur of motion. He fluttered his wings and wobbled against both his siblings while he forced himself to stand. All at once, he stood up.

Sunshine almost fell backward out of the tree in shocked surprise. Right before her eyes, the one-legged baby stood straight up in the nest.

She gasped and stared in total disbelief.

But there he stood on one leg, his right wing stretched out across the edge of the nest while his other wing pressed against his sister's back for balance. He was using his wings to balance!

"Baby! You did it!" Sunshine gasped.

Just as suddenly, he sat right back down. But he sat down; he didn't fall.

She blinked her eyes rapidly, trying to make sure she had really seen the event and not dreamed it.

In the next moment, the baby stood back up on his single leg, pressing his wings against the nest and his sister for support. And for the next few moments, he repeated this exercise over and over

63

again to the astonishment of not only Sunshine but also his two siblings.

As the baby continued sitting down and standing back up, Treetop flew up with a big, juicy bug in his beak, but he promptly dropped the bug to the ground as he joined the others in open-mouthed astonishment.

"Wha-what's going on?" Treetop finally managed to ask, his voice choked with emotion.

"Our baby is standing up!" Sunshine said with tears of joy.

"I-I see that." Treetop's head nodded up and down as he followed the baby's motions.

They all noticed how he used his wings to balance himself, but they also noticed that with each repetition his balance got better and better. At one point, he simply spread his wings apart without touching anything.

"Why is he doing that?" Treetop wondered out loud as the baby repeated his motions faster and faster.

"You taught him, Daddy! You always go up and down!" the other two shouted with glee.

"Oh yeah," Treetop muttered. "You're right! I did keep standing and sitting back down over and over, showing him how to do it. He's doing it *just like Dad*!"

All three babies laughed out loud.

"I can't believe it!" Sunshine cried joyously.

"I never thought to tell him to use his wings to push against the nest or the others to help get his balance. I thought that would be the wrong way."

Treetop shook his head with wonder. "I was wrong.

"No, you did your best, honey," Sunshine said. "He obviously learned something from you. But being just a baby, he has to use his wings that way to start learning how to balance. He'll learn soon enough how to balance like you tried to show him."

"Wow... you did it, Sunshine," Treetop whispered in awe.

"We did it. Together, we helped him learn how to stand." Sunshine smiled.

"Yes, I guess we did do it!" Treetop said softly.

"We can do always do more together than we ever could by ourselves. That's why we're mates." Sunshine leaned against Treetop, and he put his wing around her.

"That's why we're a family," he added.

"Whenever one of us needs help, the rest of the family will come to their aid. That's what families do. We help each other. We love each other," she whispered fervently.

"We're a family," Treetop said.

"We must never forget that." Sunshine sighed happily.

Sunshine and Treetop smiled down on their three babies.

The one-legged baby stood up and flapped his wings vigorously.

"That little bird there is going to learn how to fly real soon!" Sunshine winked at the smallest baby.

The baby opened his beak and smiled back at her.

"We want to learn how to fly too!" the other two shouted.

"All Mama's babies are going to learn how to fly!" Sunshine laughed.

The three babies cheered in reply.

For the rest of that sixth day, Sunshine and Treetop continued their duty as parents -- feeding the babies and protecting the nest.

Newfound joy now lifted their hearts high into the sky, almost as if they could fly forever and never touch the ground. Again and again, they brought their babies bugs and worms. They still fed them the same way, Treetop feeding the larger boy and girl while Sunshine fed the smallest baby simultaneously. They were afraid to change the routine now, even though the little baby had finally learned to stand on one leg.

But he was soon holding himself up for longer periods of time while Sunshine joyously fed him.

Their world was one of happiness once again.

That night, the two parents slept peacefully for the first since before the babies were born. The entire family slept deeply and soundly while the fireflies danced in the summer darkness and the eerie cries of the cicadas echoed in the night.

At long last, the night sky began to lighten, heralding a new day. It was the seventh day since the babies hatched. The 'Naming Day' for Treetop and Sunshine's newest babies had finally arrived.

Chapter Seven

"Are you nervous?"

Sunshine watched her mate's expression more than she waited for his response. She could always tell when Treetop was nervous -- he swallowed over and over again. She smiled as his eyes met hers.

"No, I'm not," he answered. "I'm ready for all the relatives to arrive."

"I am too. I think." Sunshine smiled nervously.

"Don't worry. The relatives will watch while we name the babies, and then they'll 'ooh' and 'ah' over the babies and tell us how much they look like us. And they'll be off again. Next time we see them, we'll be flying around with the babies."

"I'll be glad when they leave the nest," Sunshine said. "That will be a grand day."

"Don't wish your life away," Treetop said with a smile.

"Let's go over the ceremony one more time with the babies. I don't want anything to go wrong." A look of deep concern crossed Sunshine's face.

"We've done it twice this morning," Treetop protested.

"Please," Sunshine pleaded with a twinkle in her eye.

Treetop rolled his eyes, but he smiled and promptly hopped back over to the nest. Three baby mockingbirds looked up at him with silent eagerness on their faces, and he smiled down at them.

67

"Very soon, all our relatives will gather in our nest tree. They will perch on all the limbs overlooking the nest while your mother and I stand on either side of you. It is important that you wait for my cue before any of you stand up. Do you understand that so far?" Treetop gazed from one baby to the other.

"Yes, Daddy!" all three chirped excitedly.

"Good. Now, the first hatched is the first named, and that's you." Treetop nodded at the oldest male.

He nodded eagerly with understanding.

"Good. I will ask you to stand, and then I will name you."

"Will Mama name us too?" his daughter peeped.

"No, she wants me to name each of you in this brood." He glanced at Sunshine. "That's right?" he asked her as confirmation.

"Yes, yes. I'd like you to name all the babies this time," she said breathlessly. Inside, she felt a flutter of panic. For some reason, she felt something was going to go wrong. She felt impending doom approaching, but she couldn't imagine what it might be.

"So, I have picked out names for all three of you which I will bestow on each in turn, as is the way of all birds," Treetop said succinctly. "I will ask each of you to stand one at a time. Once I bestow your name, you will seat yourself and I will name the next baby. Do you understand?"

"Yes! Yes!" all three chirped excitedly.

"And once I have named each of you, so you will be known by all birds the rest of your life."

Treetop took a breath and looked over at Sunshine.

Sunshine smiled nervously back at him.

The summer sun rose steadily in the sky. As the gleaming orb rose above the treetops, mockingbirds began to arrive at the dogwood tree and perch in the limbs above the parents and their hatchlings. The branches were soon lined with mockingbirds happily twittering and chattering to each other in celebration of the 'Naming Day.' They were naturally excited to meet the latest members of the mockingbird clan that lived in this suburb and the nearby fields and forests.

"Look at those beautiful babies!" Aunty Coldrain chirped to the other birds around her.

"My, yes, doesn't the girl look just like Sunshine," Uncle Morningbreeze said.

"And the oldest male is the splitting image of Treetop," cousin Brightsun added.

Sunshine felt her nervousness growing with each new mockingbird that perched in the tree. It seemed that every mockingbird they knew was coming to this particular 'Naming Day'. She felt her stomach rumble with somersaults.

She swallowed nervously.

They were all there -- cousins and uncles and aunts and second cousins and even fifth and sixth cousins. The branches were lined with mockingbirds from end to end.

Sunshine grew dizzy while the chorus of chatter

grew louder and louder.

"Welcome, family and friends!" Treetop called out loudly with wings spread.

Sunshine felt a wave of relief -- finally, it was time to start.

"My mate, Sunshine." Treetop gazed lovingly at her.

An incredible warmth spread inside her heart. His confidence gave her a new sense of hope. Sunshine spread her wings in welcome as she and Treetop stepped slowly forward.

"Welcome, all!" Treetop shouted again to the silent throng as he and Sunshine stood still.

"Hey, Treetop! Looks like you and the missus got another beautiful brood!" Cousin Warmnight shouted joyfully.

Treetop nodded and smiled, but he held his wings up for silence.

"Our hatchlings are now seven days old. As is the way of all birds, we will name each today. By each name we bestow, so shall all birds know these hatchlings. When they take flight and wherever they may fly, as we name them today, so shall they be known to all!"

A chorus of cheers and chirps erupted throughout the branches of the dogwood tree. All throughout the other trees and yards, birds of every kind paused and looked over at the joyful shouts and realized a happy event was taking place.

Every morning and every evening was also a happy time that inspired song. All birds sang joyously at the hope a new day brought as well as when the red sun set in the west, welcoming a night of rest. Such joyous times fulfilled the oldest proverb of all the birds… *Every bird sings when they're happy!*

Often when birds heard a chorus of happy calls, they would realize some shared happiness was taking place, and many times that sound was contagious.

The happy cries of the mockingbirds had just that effect. Moments later, birds of all kinds sang out in joyful response until birdsong filled the air in every direction.

Treetop and Sunshine felt their hearts beating with pride. They glanced at each other a moment in their shared joy.

And then, it was time.

Treetop hopped closer to the nest and looked down at the oldest male, who looked back at his father with a happy smile.

"Stand up, firstborn," Treetop said with a deep and serious tone.

The baby looked over at his siblings a brief moment, and then he looked at the myriad of birds that filled every branch in the tree. He gulped nervously.

Sunshine felt her heart flutter in panic, but the baby stood up.

Treetop smiled.

"You are the firstborn. I have fed you and cared for you these past days. I see good things ahead for you, young one. You will grow strong and one day find a mate of your own. Your songs will fill the

air. And so, I bestow upon you the name ...
Cloudshadow."

A happy hush filled the air.

"Yes, many of us have known the joy of chasing
a cloud's shadow when we were young, especially
our hatching year. I bestow this name upon you in
the hope you will bring such joy to others and you
will know such joy all your life."

Every mockingbird sang out enthusiastically in
response.

Treetop nodded.

Cloudshadow dutifully sat down, his beak
parted in a happy smile.

"Stand up, secondborn." Treetop paused. "And
our only daughter of this hatching."

Sunshine watched as her daughter looked
around at all the birds surrounding them, but
without pause, she rose quickly at her mother's
silent urging.

"You look so much like your mother," Treetop
began with warmth. "Of all our daughters, you
resemble most my lovely mate."

Sunshine smiled proudly when Treetop turned
to her.

He smiled. "You already chirp and call out with
happiness that warms your mother's heart as well as
mine. You've already brought happiness and joy to
us, and you haven't even left the nest!"

Shouts of applause filled the tree.

"And so, I bestow upon you a name that I
believe you will fulfill, even as you have already. I
look forward to hearing your sweet voice join the

morning chorus. I am sure your songs will bring joy to others just as you have brought joy to us already. I bestow upon you the name ... Songjoy!"

Shouts and songs filled the tree and spilled over yard after yard throughout the subdivision as every bird once again raised its voice in unison, and a new wave of birdsong filled the air.

Sunshine felt a sense of relief that the ceremony was almost over. She felt something else stirring inside her as well, for now, the smallest baby would be given a name.

She felt a profound sense of relief just in the fact that he had lived to see this day. She shook her head. So many times she had feared she would return to the nest and find this baby dead. That fear had filled her heart with dread until it tainted every other thought and feeling for days on end.

But now, Treetop would name this baby too.

Treetop nodded, and Songjoy sat down.

He now nodded down at the smallest baby. The baby smiled back with eager expectation.

"Stand up, final born."

The smallest baby stood up quickly, but as he did so, he almost lost his balance. He quickly extended his wing across Songjoy's back and steadied himself.

Getting his balance, he stood up straight and tall.

Sunshine felt it before she heard anything. Dark foreboding filled her being. At first, she couldn't understand why the happiness of the moment had changed in a single heartbeat.

Harsh, critical whispers whipped like a strong wind all around her.

She looked around at the others and now noticed their shocked expressions. Her own heart skipped a beat as she finally heard some of what they were whispering.

"He's only got one leg!"

"What's wrong with him? Oh... Oh! He's deformed!"

"It must be... 'Death-on-the-Wind!"

"Yeeeesss. Lots of eggs have failed to hatch this season.."

"Ohhh, it scares me to look at him..."

Sunshine felt so dizzy. The whispering intensified...

"How can he stand on one leg? It's so... so weird..."

"He looks so funny."

"Isn't he strange."

"It's kind of scary..."

Sunshine felt her heart sink with despair. She looked over at Treetop. Like her, he was looking around helplessly as the cacophony of harsh whispers came at them like a tidal wave.

He swallowed nervously and averted his eyes.

Some of the birds stared in silent shock while others seemed to draw back as if horrified.

Sunshine now felt angry. What was the matter with them? He was a normal bird -- except he only had one leg.

Treetop looked back at the baby, whose happy countenance was now replaced by frightened puzzlement.

Sunshine hopped over to the other side of the nest and stood beside Treetop. "Continue with the ceremony, Treetop. Name the last baby."

Treetop looked at her with a fearful expression. He shook his head silently as if in defeat.

Or was it embarrassment?

"Treetop, what's wrong with that baby?" Aunty Coldrain called out clearly.

"Nothing. I mean, he was born with only one leg ... but otherwise he's fine." Treetop's voice sounded weak and unsure.

"I've heard of other babies born with problems this season." Coldrain now turned away from Treetop and addressed all the gathered birds. "Something is in the air, something bad."

"Death-on-the-Wind!" several said together in a hush of fearfulness.

"Last season too, there was a rash of eggs that never hatched!" a frightened voice cried out.

Sunshine felt a chill. She too remembered all the sad parents last season, crying over their unborn babies. Even she and Treetop had not been immune. In their second nesting last season, two of the three eggs had not hatched. She remembered her shock, for it was the first time such a tragedy had happened to them.

"I've heard that the chickadees had a number of deformed babies born this season too!" another bird shouted.

"And I've heard the same thing from the cardinals!"

"Robin parents are reporting babies born with problems -- and all die soon after birth."

"Death-on-the-Wind!"

"For two seasons now, there have been many unhatched eggs, babies never born!" added another.

Sunshine felt like crying. She looked down at the still unnamed baby. Her heart hurt as she saw his frightened eyes pleading to her.

He didn't know what to do, and he didn't have a name! And yet, he continued to stand tall and straight on his one leg, waiting for his name.

"Bestow his name," Sunshine whispered urgently to Treetop, but he appeared lost in thought. He continued to stand there, just staring back at all the birds as they either stared at the one-legged baby or else chattered among themselves, oblivious to everything else.

The ceremony was falling apart.

Anger filled Sunshine, but she also felt a new determination. "I will name the baby."

Every bird suddenly stopped in mid-sentence. All eyes fixed on her and the one-legged baby.

Sunshine nodded confidently. When she looked down at her youngest baby and caught his eye, the baby's expression of fear and uncertainty was instantly replaced with a happy smile.

"Are you ready, my youngest baby?"

The baby nodded excitedly, but Sunshine's heart dropped. All above her, the whispers began again.

"You can't name that baby," Aunt Coldrain said with a cold and condescending tone.

"What do you mean, I can't name this baby?"

Sunshine shot back angrily.

Coldrain hopped down between Sunshine and Treetop.

Treetop looked from one to the other in silent consternation. His continued silence and indecision hurt Sunshine even more than the cruel whispers of the others. She wished with all her soul that he would gather himself and take charge, but he remained silent before the critical stares of everyone.

"I mean…" She leaned closer to Sunshine and whispered the rest of her words. "I mean, obviously this baby will die soon. How can you give him a name? It will just make his death that much more painful."

"Get back to your branch!" Sunshine shouted.

"Well! You don't have to be so rude." Coldrain shrugged at Sunshine. "I'm only trying to help."

"No, you're not helping at all." Sunshine looked up at the other birds. "And the rest of you, quit your whispering. I shall name this baby myself!"

The whispers stopped, but the heartless stares continued.

Sunshine hated their stares, their haughty, condescending expressions, and again, she caught snatches of what they whispered to each other as the murmuring slowly returned.

"He looks so queer."

"He's so… *different*."

"And he's so skinny -- *don't they feed him?*"

She turned back to face her baby, who once

again smiled joyfully under her loving gaze.

In spite of the whispers that surrounded him and all the rude stares focused on his missing leg, he stood bravely before her. His eyes saw only her now, she could tell. He parted his beak ever so slightly and smiled back at her, ignoring everyone else.

His strength somehow gave her strength, and she realized that their shared love somehow gave each of them power.

"You are our final born, little one. You have fought harder than most to get to this day. Your life has been one of challenge, but you have conquered all these challenges so far, and I am positive you will continue to meet all the challenges life will throw at you -- and there will be many."

Sunshine paused.

"Life will not be easy for you, but you will learn to fly higher than most birds, and you will fly to new heights which no bird has ever known -- just because of who you are."

A hush fell upon the tree as all the mockingbirds listened with outright disbelief.

"How can a one-legged bird do all *that*?" Coldrain shouted with disdain.

Sunshine ignored her. "I bestow upon you the name ... Bluesky!"

Now the hush changed to a collective gasp of utter disbelief.

Treetop finally found his voice. "You can't name him that!" he cried out.

"I just did."

"That name is… special. It's reserved!"

"Reserved for who?"

"For birds destined for greatness!"

"Then, this little bird will accomplish greatness!" Sunshine's eyes narrowed in challenge at Treetop.

Treetop shook his head with exasperation. "How can that be? He's only got one leg."

"He's already beaten the odds -- he's survived to his 'Naming Day!'"

"What can a one-legged bird do?" Treetop bent his head down and groaned.

"Everyone has a song to sing." Sunshine replied firmly, and yet her voice was full of hope. "And Bluesky will add his own unique voice to the 'Song of Life.'"

Treetop closed his eyes as if he were in pain -- but Sunshine realized it was a pain of the heart.

"Every bird has something special inside -- and this baby is no different, even if he only has one leg." Sunshine watched her mate closely, hoping against hope her words were getting through to him.

Treetop opened his eyes and hopped slowly away from the nest. He nodded at the nest and spoke to her in a solemn tone. "Then, name him anything you like. But not Bluesky," he said with somberness.

Sunshine felt so alone, as if Treetop were abandoning her and this little baby before all the onlookers. She felt so alone, as if it were just she and this small baby standing against the world.

She focused on Bluesky's tiny face as he looked

79

hopefully up at her. Once again, he smiled innocently. She felt her heart flutter with deep emotion.

"I will not change it." Forcing everything else aside, she smiled proudly down at Bluesky, and Bluesky smiled with love back at his mother.

She looked up at all the mockingbirds staring at them from the branches. "He shall be known as Bluesky to all birds wherever he may fly! Every place he goes, to every bird he meets, he shall be known as Bluesky, and may he bring hope to all!" Sunshine shouted with unmitigated pride.

Not a single bird spoke and not a single bird sang out, but the harsh whispers started again.

"The ceremony is over," Sunshine added.

One by one, the mockingbirds flew away. As they left, most cast a silent stare at the one-legged mockingbird still standing straight and stalwart in the nest.

She had forgotten to instruct him sit down, but now she felt it best he continue standing before them all as they took flight. He would show them all. He was just as good as any of them!

Cloudshadow and Songjoy remained sitting in the nest beside their brother.

Sunshine tried to ignore the odd stares leveled at Bluesky. As she focused on the nest and its three occupants, she realized that their feathers were now the colors of a fully grown mockingbird. They would grow even more quickly in the next few days -- and soon they would leave the nest.

When Sunshine laughed out loud at that happy

thought, Cloudshadow, Songjoy, and Bluesky each smiled up at her.

Sunshine felt a stirring in her heart. In spite of the intolerance and prejudice against her one baby, she realized all she needed was right here -- her babies and her mate.

But as she looked up at Treetop, her heart burned with fear again.

Treetop stared blankly, lost inside his boiling emotions and his troubled thoughts. He seemed different somehow. He had been deeply affected by the overwhelming reaction of their relatives -- by their shocked stares and rude whispers and at their revulsion of the little one-legged baby.

He seemed lost somehow. He seemed almost afraid.

It made her feel afraid, deep inside.

She looked back down at her three babies. Once again, she felt her inner strength return. All they needed was each other. She would have to reassure Treetop of this truth as well.

Even if every mockingbird in the world rejected their baby, they would love him -- they would love each other.

Love would conquer all!

Chapter Eight

Cloudshadow hopped nimbly out of the nest.

Bluesky stared in shocked surprise as Cloudshadow took several steps out on the limb. The little mockingbird spread his wings as if testing the air a moment and then walked confidently farther and farther away.

Sitting beside him in the nest, Songjoy looked from Cloudshadow back to Bluesky with a puzzled expression.

The three babies were now fourteen days old. Their feathers were completely grown out. In fact, their wings displayed the familiar black and white barred coloration of their parents and the plumage over their body was dark gray with whitish-gray on the breast. All three babies were miniature versions of their parents now.

Bluesky, however, was the exception in two ways. He was obviously more diminutive than his two siblings, almost a third smaller than Cloudshadow, and of course, as he stood with his neck craned to keep an eye on Cloudshadow, who walked farther away from the nest, he stood on only one leg.

"Where are you going?" Bluesky shouted after him.

"The nest is too crowded," Cloudshadow called back. "Besides, I'm ready to learn how to fly!"

Songjoy flapped her wings with a sudden burst of energy, almost as if she wanted to go straight from the nest into the air!

Her wings caught Bluesky by surprise. He wobbled off-balance a moment and with a 'ka-plomp' fell over on his side into the bottom of the nest.

"Hey! You knocked me over!" Bluesky protested.

Songjoy laughed a moment. She settled again into the bottom of the nest as she and Bluesky eyed Cloudshadow standing way out on the limb.

Bluesky struggled to get his body just right so he could balance himself with his wings and get his leg directly underneath his body. While he squirmed for position, his sister kept pushing back against his wings even as he used her for leverage.

"Stop pushing on me! I'll tell Dad when he gets back!"

Bluesky continued his efforts; it was the only way he could get himself just right before he could stand. Finally, he felt himself ready.

He stood effortlessly, holding his wings out for balance.

Songjoy now moved to the opposite side of the nest. She stared at Bluesky a moment with frustration but quickly remembered the newfound adventure of Cloudshadow.

"You better come back here! Mom's going to be mad if you fall out of the tree!" Songjoy chided.

"I'm not going to fall out," Cloudshadow shot back. "You're just jealous that I've left the nest first!"

"No, I'm not!"

"Yes, you are!"

"No! I... am... not!" Songjoy said each word slowly and with an edge to her voice.

"Then, come on out with me!" Cloudshadow challenged. He smiled widely. "There's nothing to it."

Songjoy's eyes widened.

"Come on."

"No, I'd better wait on Mama."

"You're just scared!"

"No, I'm not."

"Yeah, you're scared, just like little bitty Bluesky." Cloudshadow's challenging tone now changed to a taunt.

"I am not scared!" Bluesky said firmly.

"Then prove it."

"Well, okay." Bluesky hopped over to the edge of the nest as Songjoy scrambled out of his way.

"D-do you think you should leave the nest without Mom and Dad here?" Songjoy asked fearfully.

"I'll be all right. Cloudshadow's all right, isn't he?"

"Yes, b-but..."

Bluesky started hopping higher and higher in the air as he gauged the height of the edge of the nest and the limb beyond, trying to guess how far he would need to jump up and over to get to it. He hopped a little higher each time until with a mighty bound he leapt up and forward over the edge of the nest.

He guessed wrong.

His toes caught on the nest, and he fell forward onto the limb right on his face.

As he flapped his wings in shock and fright, his body started to slip over the rounded side of the tree limb.

"Bluesky!" His mother shouted with horror.

He stopped his frantic motions at hearing his mother's voice above him. Slowly, he turned his head and body and pulled his leg away from some of the tiny sticks of the nest that had snagged him.

Now fully outside the nest, he lay partly on his side with his leg awkwardly bent behind him.

"Ah, Mom. You scared me."

"Bluesky." Her tone was a mixture of fear and surprise. "What are you doing?"

"I'm leaving the nest. All birds leave the nest -- eventually. That's what you and Dad told us just yesterday."

"But, but... you're not ready!"

Bluesky started squirming in order to bring his leg back underneath his body so he could stand, but he found it more difficult now. As he fought for position, he realized he had nothing on which he could lean on for leverage like he had back in the nest. Even worse, he no longer had his sister right next to him to use for leverage. After he struggled in vain a few minutes, he sighed loudly and looked around.

He saw his dad now perched beside his mom two branches above him. Their anxious stares made him feel uncomfortable.

"W-what's he doing?" Treetop asked with

surprise.

"He's leaving the nest, bumble-head. What does it look like he's doing," Sunshine retorted.

"I-I," Treetop stuttered. He swallowed deeply. "If he's not careful, he's going to fall o--"

"Shhhhhh!" Sunshine replied. "You're making him nervous."

"What are we going to do?" Treetop asked.

Sunshine looked at Treetop with deep concern etched across her face. "I don't know."

"Ah, Mom. Don't worry." Bluesky shook his head with exasperation.

Pressing his right wing down on the branch, Bluesky stretched his neck so he could get a better look at everything.

He noted that even though the tree limb on which he lay was about half the width of nest, the bark was rough and filled with grooves. He knew if he could get himself positioned just right and stand up, his toenails would easily grab onto the bark and help him keep his balance.

The big question was how could he get himself up?

Suddenly, his eye was drawn to a smaller branch growing out the top of the main branch a couple of inches away. He realized if he used that small branch for leverage by placing one wing against it, he could get himself in position to stand.

With renewed effort, he squirmed toward it.

He ignored the gasps from his parents above him. He knew they could do nothing to help him now. He had left the nest -- and that was that.

Bluesky used his wing to drag himself slowly forward. He started to slip over the side again but quickly adjusted his weight and pressed with his wing against the limb underneath him until he regained his hold.

He heard more gasps all around as Songjoy and Cloudshadow joined his parents.

Nobody thought he could do it, but he'd show them.

Finally, after what seemed like an eternity, he made it to the small branch growing up out of the limb. Twisting his body while he pressed his right wing against the small branch for support, he inched his body around. It was a lot harder here outside the nest, but as he got used to the rough surface of the limb and used it for leverage as much as the tiny branch on which he supported part of his body, his sense of balance finally returned. With a final twist of his body, he worked his leg under his body.

He stood up.

"Oh, Bluesky!" Sunshine closed her eyes as her entire body swayed in circles. "I think I'm going to faint."

"See, he did it. I knew he could," Cloudshadow said with a smile.

"You did it!" Songjoy shouted with glee, and with a bound, she hopped over the side of the nest and walked quickly up to Bluesky.

Bluesky blinked in amazement at how easily she crossed the same distance it had taken him several minutes to cover. He panted from his strenuous efforts.

"I'm going around you." In a flash of feathers, she walked around Bluesky, pressing against his body so hard he felt himself getting off-balance again.

"Songjoy!" Treetop and Sunshine shouted simultaneously.

Bluesky flapped his wings for balance a moment and leaned against the small branch. He felt his strength, and even more important, his confidence returning. After a few more deep breaths, he hopped around the branch and joined Cloudshadow and Songjoy. The three turned to their parents, who continued to stare in shock and surprise down at them.

"Feed me! Feed me!" they all shouted together.

Sunshine and Treetop looked at each other.

"Well, they've left nest." Treetop shook his head with amazement.

Sunshine looked down at her three juvenile mockers. "My babies are growing up!"

"Yes, they'll be flying soon," Treetop added.

Sunshine covered her face with her wings. "I don't know if I can handle all that in one day."

"Oh, they'll have to get their courage up before they do that. Remember, the first time is the hardest." Treetop chuckled at the memory of his first flight.

"How do we learn to fly, Dad?" Cloudshadow shouted.

"Yeah, how do we learn?" Bluesky added enthusiastically, as if he were ready to do it right then.

"It's easy!" Treetop laughed.

"Oh, honey, not now," Sunshine pleaded, but Treetop ignored her concern at this happy juncture in the growth of the babies. Across his gray face, his eyes sparkled with pride for his three babies.

"C'mon, Dad, tell us," Songjoy pleaded. "I want to fly too."

Treetop smiled down at them and spoke with a chipper tone. "All you have to do is leap off the branch and flap your wings!"

Bluesky leaned over the edge of limb and looked down. The ground was so far down it made his head dizzy.

"Wow, it's a long way down," Cloudshadow said with a hint of fear. "What if I can't fly? What if I fall down?"

"You've got wings," Treetop said simply. "When you're ready, it'll be easy."

Bluesky, Songjoy, and Cloudshadow looked at each other with puzzled expressions. Then they each spread their wings apart and flapped furiously a moment. A few small feathers sailed free and began to fall in lazy circles down to the ground far, far below.

All three babies stopped flapping and watched the slow descent of their feathers with a solemn intensity. Long seconds later, the feathers gently settled to the ground.

"Wow, it is a long way down the ground," Cloudshadow said with sudden conviction. He looked up at his parents. "I think I like it up here on this branch just fine."

Chapter Nine

The darkness gradually and almost imperceptibly grew lighter, and one by one, the stars disappeared from the sky. Morning approached, although the sun's blazing rim had not yet risen above the distant horizon.

Bluesky slept next to his siblings while his mother and father slept two branches above them. As the sky continued to lighten by small degrees, Bluesky's eyes fluttered open.

He smiled at the semi-darkness, recognizing the growing lightness in the sky. His senses told him morning approached, but he waited with rising expectation for the sure sign morning had arrived.

Somewhere in the unseen distance, a thrasher sang out joyfully. A few seconds later, a cardinal chirped cheerily with the happy voice unique to its kind.

Bluesky knew the morning chorus was merely tuning up.

Now a family of song sparrows added their clear, happy trills. As they continued to sing, catbirds, towhees, wrens, robins, bluebirds, tufted titmice, chickadees, warblers, finches, and several other kinds of birds added their own distinctive voices.

The morning air filled with bird song.

In that special time when night was fast fading away and the increasing light revealed the sky above, the birds sang in chorus much as they had since the beginning of time. Whether it was their inner pleasure in welcoming a new day or their happiness in simply being alive, the myriad songs, chirps, trills, warbles, and whistles blended together and permeated the world like a joyful symphony.

Every morning this same joyous symphony emanated from every bird living in every corner of the world -- for those awake early enough to listen and enjoy their majestic performance.

Bluesky watched carefully as the world slowly revealed itself in all its morning glory.

He and his siblings had left the nest two days ago, and now the third morning was beginning around them.

His parents now fed them from the tree branch on which they lived. Each parent would return from their hunting, and Cloudshadow and Songjoy would quickly walk to them in order to get their portions. It wasn't so easy for Bluesky. He would hop as quickly as he could to join them, but his siblings always beat him there. However, his parents made it a point to land closer to him so he could get the first juicy morsels from time to time.

All of them slept comfortably on the branch. Bluesky discovered he could somehow keep his balance even while asleep, gripping the branch tightly while roosting peacefully. He soon realized that with each passing day he could hop and bounce on the branches of the tree with greater ease than the day before.

During the day, his siblings ran up and down the branches playing with each other and with him, although there was no way he could hop fast enough to keep up with either of them. He did his best, hopping over obstacles such as small branches and leaves in his efforts to keep up. They chided him for his slowness, but he took it in stride -- life was fun and happy right now.

His siblings had roughhoused and even inadvertently pushed against him at times in their play as they ran up and down the branches. He had almost fallen off several times.

The way his mom gasped at times, it seemed he'd almost fallen off a hundred times.

He felt the movement of Songjoy and Cloudshadow as they awakened to the growing chorus around them. In quick succession, both yawned.

"Okay, kids. Mom and I are off to hunt for breakfast. Stay close -- we'll be back soon."

With a flurry of movement, Treetop and Sunshine took flight. They shot between the dense network of leaves and branches and disappeared into the distance beyond.

Bluesky, Songjoy, and Cloudshadow raised themselves erect and flapped their wings vigorously in imitation of their parents, but as the two adult mockingbirds disappeared from view, the three juvenile mockers settled down.

"I'm hungry," Cloudshadow said earnestly.

"Me too. I hope Mom and Dad find some tasty bugs fast," Songjoy added.

Bluesky hopped a couple of feet away and again flapped his wings with renewed energy. He felt his wings growing stronger each time he exercised them this way. Inside his feathery breast, his heart thumped rapid-fire.

"Hey, what are you going to do, Bluesky? You gonna fly off and help Mom and Dad?" Cloudshadow and Songjoy laughed heartily at Cloudshadow's query.

Bluesky smiled back at them, not offended by their jest at all. In fact, the more they talked about flying and the stronger his wings felt, the stronger his desire grew to fly off into the sky like all the other birds.

He flapped his wings with even greater effort until suddenly he felt himself lifting off the branch!

Instantly, he folded his wings back to rest against his sides with a fearful expression in his eyes. The sudden realization that he had almost taken off filled him with both fear and yearning.

"Whoa!" Cloudshadow gasped in surprise. "You actually came off the branch a little bit that time."

"What did it feel like?" Songjoy asked excitedly. "What did it feel like?" She paused as she noticed the strange expression on Bluesky's face. "Was it… scary?"

Bluesky tried to sort out the feelings exploding inside his pounding heart, but they were so confusing!

"It was kind of scary, and… and exciting all at the same time!" Bluesky blurted out the last with a burst of emotion.

"Do you think you'll fly today?" Songjoy asked

with a sincere tone.

"I'm not sure."

"Well, I just might fly today myself," Cloudshadow said with an air of importance. Obviously, he didn't want to be outdone by his little brother. He flapped his wings energetically to add emphasis to his intentions, but he didn't quite lift off the branch.

"You didn't even lift up!" Bluesky taunted good-naturedly.

"Yeah, you aren't scared, are you?" Songjoy added.

"Of course not!" Cloudshadow shot back. Now, he flapped his wings harder than ever -- and suddenly, Cloudshadow lifted up into the air just above the branch.

"Ahhhh!" Cloudshadow yelled in fright as he fell back onto the branch. He lost his balance and tottered over the edge a moment before he waved his wings wildly and got himself back on it.

"Wow!" Bluesky and Songjoy shouted together.

"I'm going to try." Songjoy fluffed out her feathers and placed her legs in position. She checked the area all around her with a quick glance to make sure all was to her liking. Then, with a sudden burst, she jumped upward and flapped her wings with all her might in an excellent imitation of her parents.

As both their beaks dropped open, Bluesky and Cloudshadow watched in shocked awe as Songjoy flew away.

For the first few feet, Songjoy's flying was strong, but as soon as she realized she was flying, her body wobbled and her wings lost their rhythmic motion. She started falling, and this caused her to beat her wings harder -- though not in a coordinated or controlled manner.

Shrieking, Songjoy flew into a thick clump of leaves. Several leaves exploded into the air as she reached out with both legs and latched hold with her tiny claws. She skidded to a quick halt and perched, panting.

"Wow!" Bluesky and Cloudshadow shouted together.

"You flew to the other side of the tree!" Bluesky was impressed with his sister's feat.

Cloudshadow's eyes widened. "Wow! She did, didn't she!"

Bluesky and Cloudshadow looked at each other a moment.

"All right, I ain't gonna let my little sister outdo me!" Cloudshadow fluffed his feathers out and stretched his wings as he readied himself. He cast a glance at Bluesky.

"Well, go on," Bluesky said.

"I am," Cloudshadow said with just a hint of fear.

"Hey, I can see the man house from here really good," Songjoy said, unseen from the other side of the tree.

That was just the incentive Cloudshadow required.

Cloudshadow bent his legs and launched

himself upward, beating his wings with steady motions. He leapt forward and quickly realized the protective feeling of the branch underneath his body was gone -- only the distant ground was visible far below.

Cloudshadow beat his wings faster!

He tried to direct his flight toward the branch where Songjoy landed, *but flying was harder than it looked.*

He found himself suddenly beyond the outer branches of the dogwood tree. With a gasp, he realized he was high in the air with nothing below him.

He turned quickly and headed back to the tree, losing altitude the entire time. Cloudshadow lost his rhythm, and his flapping motions grew more desperate. He screamed as he flew into the leaves just like his sister.

Bluesky peered down at the lowest branch almost directly below where Songjoy now perched. Cloudshadow gripped that branch with all his might with both his eyes tightly clenched.

"Is it over?" Cloudshadow finally asked.

"Is what over?" Songjoy asked.

"Is my life over? Did I die?" Cloudshadow kept his eyes shut.

"Nope. You survived." Songjoy giggled.

"But you *almost* died!" Bluesky laughed. "Just a little bit farther and…wham!"

Songjoy's tinkling laughter joined Bluesky's hearty guffaws.

"It ain't funny," Cloudshadow retorted as he

checked himself to make sure he was indeed alive. "If you're so brave, why don't you fly, Bluesky!"

Bluesky suddenly realized he was all alone on the branch. He heard Songjoy's voice, but now she was way on the other side of the tree, and he could barely see Cloudshadow down below.

With renewed determination, Bluesky bent his leg just as he had seen the others do, and without a second thought, he launched himself upward, flapping his wings.

It was truly wonderful -- just as Mom said it would be.

He felt the air brushing against his face and feathers with a refreshing tingle. He managed, although a bit awkwardly, to fly between two clumps of leaves and up and over another branch. With every passing second, he felt more and more comfortable, and his flapping motions grew more and more fluid and steady.

Bluesky felt at home in the air. He instantly realized that flying was much easier than trying to hop on one leg!

His heart fluttered with excitement as he felt his body magically lifted on the invisible folds of the wind. The golden circle of the sun blazed high above his head in a clear blue sky sprinkled with white, puffy clouds. He felt so free. He felt so happy. He felt so powerful!

Just as suddenly, he realized how much he missed having the sure footing of the branch under him as protection. His wing motion grew erratic as he also realized he was really far away from the tree itself, much less its comforting branches.

He was falling.

Actually, it was more a semi-controlled and awkward descent at full speed.

He flew clumsily in his panic, his jerky movements causing him to shift his body weight first right and then left. At times he found himself lifting upward as he almost regained the rhythm of flight again, only to have panic cloud his mind and throw him into another rapid decent.

The rapid descents quickly outnumbered the brief ascents, and then Bluesky landed with a soft 'thump' in the grass right in the middle of the backyard.

He extended his wings against the soft grass in an effort to push himself up. He found it easy, since the blades of grass all around him bent but also provided leverage. He stood quickly and surveyed his new surroundings, but even as he stood, he found he needed to flutter his wings in order to help maintain his balance.

He saw the gigantic man house first. The huge structure seemed to fill part of the sky far above him. Bluesky turned his head and saw the dogwood tree from which he had just flown. From his new perspective, it too seemed to fill a large part of the sky and the world in that direction.

Everything seemed so much bigger from down here on the ground.

Movement caught his eye. He realized it was a bug -- a delicious kind his parents often fed him -- moving just out of his reach.

Bluesky hopped vigorously toward it, his long beak attacking like a weapon, but the bug simply spread its tiny wings and buzzed away.

Bluesky cocked his head to one side and watched it disappear into another clump of grass farther away. He calmly contemplated his next move.

Without warning, his mother landed a few feet away. She began to nonchalantly hunt bugs among the blades of grass. Bluesky watched with wide eyes -- this was the first time he had actually watched her hunt bugs!

She spread her wings out in a slow, stop-action motion. She paused briefly before extending them fully in order to startle any bugs in the grass. She walked forward two steps and repeated her motions again.

"Watch me carefully, Bluesky. This is how a mockingbird startles bugs so we can catch them," his mother said without looking up.

Bluesky fixed his gaze intently on her.

She repeated the same motions a third time, and suddenly several bugs flew up in the air just ahead of her.

She leaped toward one, snagging it out of the air with a quick stab of her beak. She quickly chewed it up and then turned toward Bluesky.

He suddenly remembered how hungry he was.

"Feed me! Feed me!" he chirped plaintively.

"Come to me," Sunshine replied.

Bluesky hopped quickly toward her until he was right beside her. She leaned over and popped the half-chewed bug into his opened beak.

Bluesky chewed appreciatively. The bug was fresh -- tasty and crunchy.

"Feed me! Feed me!" he chirped loudly.

Sunshine walked rapidly away, and Bluesky attempted to follow in a mad dash of hops and fluttering wings.

His mother turned. "Stay back a little. You'll scare the bugs before I'm ready."

Bluesky paused obediently.

Sunshine returned to her hunting, and after a few bursts of walking and wing spreading, she nabbed another bug.

"Feed me! Feed me!" Bluesky begged.

Much to his surprise, Sunshine took flight, flew a short distance, and landed in a small group of bushes. She paused on a slender branch and looked back at Bluesky.

Instinctively, Bluesky flapped his wings in imitation, but he folded them up again. He was puzzled. He wondered why his mother had fled and not even fed him. After all, he saw her catch a bug just for him!

"Come here," she chirped. "I have a nice bug for you."

She was a long way away this time. He realized he would tire himself out if he hopped all the way to her. He bent his leg and leapt upward. Bluesky spread his wings and flapped vigorously.

He surprised himself as he flew upward with relative ease. Just as quickly, he realized he was heading away from his mother and the juicy bug.

He redirected his flight to the left but found he had overcompensated. He was now heading toward the huge man house.

Bluesky corrected his awkward flight path and headed straight for the bushes.

"Ahhhh!" he cried, crashing into several pliant branches. After another soft 'thump', he found himself among some dead leaves under the thickest part of the bush.

"You're going to have to work on those landings, young bird." Sunshine laughed.

Bluesky wriggled until he got himself in position and stood up. He looked around.

"Over here."

He flew up to his mother and managed to land right next to her. He eagerly took the juicy morsel - - and this one was extra crunchy too!

"Bluesky, you've learned to fly, and you'll soon perfect that landing too." Sunshine tried to repress a giggle, but it escaped anyway.

Bluesky didn't take offense. He knew he must look funny. After all, he'd ended up on his back end on two out of three landings now.

"You've got to learn to be careful, Bluesky."

"Why, Mama?" Bluesky asked.

"Well, baby, you need to be careful when you land on the ground. Most of the world's creatures walk on the ground, and many of them would love to catch a careless bird." She leaned closer. "What did we teach you back at the nest when you land on the ground?"

"Look around first and make sure nothing is

nearby -- and then look again." Bluesky opened his beak and smiled at his accurate recollection of his parents' teaching.

"Good, and I did see you look around -- though you seemed a bit in awe more than you were making sure you were not in danger."

"Yes, Mama. I mean, I'm sorry, Mama. I've never been on the ground before."

"That's all right, but make sure you're safe first thing when you land -- look all around carefully."

"Yes, Mama!"

"Now, what especially must you beware?"

"Beware of cat!" Bluesky felt a chill of terror. He'd completely forgotten about those particular creatures and the danger they posed to birds. He looked out toward the open yard with newfound respect.

"And, what else?"

"Be *'very bewary'* of man."

"That's a good baby."

"Mama, why do we need to beware of man? Will he eat us like a cat?"

Sunshine shook her head. "No, Bluesky. Man is the strangest of all creatures. We birds fear him more because he is apt to do anything, either harm us or kill us, if we let him get too near."

"Ohhhh," Bluesky said with a bit of puzzlement.

"Now, you and your siblings have reached the next stage of life -- you can fly!"

"Yes, and it's fun too! Just like you told us!" Bluesky chirped excitedly.

"Are you Mama's 'good baby'?"

"Yes!" Bluesky responded.

"Mama doesn't want any 'bad babies.' So, watch your father and me carefully. Don't stray out of our sight."

"I won't!" Bluesky promised with a quick flap of his little wings.

Sunshine looked up at the dogwood tree. A moment later, Treetop flew down into the grass below. Sunshine flew out to join him. Together, the two parents searched diligently among the blades of grass until each had captured a juicy bug.

Each raised their prize upward and called out to Songjoy and Cloudshadow.

"Feed me! Feed me!" both little ones chirped eagerly, but Sunshine and Treetop stayed in place.

After a few moments of continued unanswered calls, the two young mockingbirds burst from the leaves of the dogwood at the same time from different branches. Each landed awkwardly near their parents, and each was quickly rewarded by the nearest parent.

For the rest of that day, Treetop and Sunshine continued to feed their three babies, but now they started a new 'game' with their babies. Like many games, this one had a teaching purpose.

The two mockingbird parents would catch a bug within sight of their babies. The babies would see the captured prize and quickly call out, asking to be fed.

Instead of taking the food to their babies, however, the parent birds would now fly farther away with their captured prize held fast in their

103

slender beaks. Sometimes they would fly up to a low branch of a nearby tree while other times they would land under a bush. There they waited, ignoring the plaintive cries of their offspring.

After a few moments, the babies realized their parents were not coming to them. The babies would then take flight and go to the parent in order to be fed the tasty morsel.

Over and over again in this crafty fashion both parents persuaded their babies to practice the art of flying, and the babies, without even realizing it, obeyed them again and again. With each flight, their confidence and skill grew.

Bluesky, Songjoy, and Cloudshadow grew steadily more proficient at both flying and especially at landing.

When the sky above finally began to darken, Treetop and Sunshine flew up into a tall poplar tree that grew near the chain link fence at the rear of the backyard. Both parents perched on one of the lower branches, well in sight of the three babies on the ground below.

"I think Mom and Dad want us to fly up there and join them," Songjoy said perceptively.

"Why do you think that?" Cloudshadow asked.

"I don't know. Well, it's just that they've done that same trick all day. They fly away and want us to follow -- like a game."

"Yeah, I like that game." Bluesky laughed.

"Well, they're a long way up there. I think I can…"

Before Cloudshadow could finish, Songjoy leapt

up and soared away toward her parents. Her flight path was not perfectly straight, but she had gotten better at correcting herself in flight and was able to land on a branch near her parents.

Bluesky and Cloudshadow heard their parents sing out with gladness.

"Maybe they do want us to fly up there with them?" Cloudshadow turned to Bluesky.

"I don't know," Bluesky replied.

"Well, I'm going up there. I'm afraid a cat might find us down here alone!"

"And Mama said that at least two cats live here," Bluesky said, recalling his mother's words. "They might be coming to get us at any time."

That was evidently enough for Cloudshadow; he flew away with a rustling of feathers and wings.

Bluesky watched in a detached manner while his brother flew to the other side of the tree from his parents. Well, at least he landed in the same tree.

Bluesky looked around, suddenly aware he was alone near the edge of the bushes that lined the side of the huge man house. He looked up at the perpendicular walls of this gigantic, wooden nest. He had never seen a man before, but Bluesky imagined that if his nest was this big, then the man himself must be a gigantic creature compared to a small bird. The little mockingbird wondered about the man creature, especially what it looked like.

Suddenly, from one of the rectangular shiny patches of the man house, a face appeared.

Bluesky felt his heart pounding in his chest as fear paralyzed him. The little mockingbird stared upward at the strange visage that stared back down at him with piercing eyes.

Bluesky's fear suddenly took over, and he leapt into the air in a blur of motion. He flew instinctively toward his old home in the dogwood tree, but as he flew higher he felt the reassurance of being surrounded by air -- there was no immediate danger to him here.

When he remembered his parents had perched in the poplar tree, Bluesky redirected his flight and soon landed on the branch below them.

As the sun set lower in the western sky, the three babies gathered together on the same branch with their parents. Soon all were fast asleep. The stars began to twinkle like thousands of tiny diamonds in the velvet night sky above the little family of mockingbirds.

Chapter Ten

Mark gazed at the young mockingbird.

He was sitting in his favorite bird-watching spot at the kitchen table, looking out the large bay window onto the back patio and the backyard. He loved to sit here and relax.

For the last few minutes his attention had been drawn to a mother mockingbird feeding one of her young who had recently left the nest. Mark could tell it was a young bird by its awkward attempts to fly and because it still begged its mother to feed him every time she captured a bug.

He laughed to himself as the small mocker fluttered its wings and cried plaintively to be fed.

Mark marveled at how the mother would seemingly ignore the baby. After a few moments of this nonsense, the baby would fly over and be rewarded with a quick meal from her.

"Mrrrrooowww."

Mark looked down as KC ambled up to join him. He knew she wanted a massage around her ears, but she also seemed to enjoy watching the birds along with him. Many a lazy weekend afternoon, KC would sit patiently beside him, and together they would watch in wonder as the birds flew to the feeders.

In fact, it seemed to Mark that KC looked longingly out at the birds, almost as if she wished she could fly like them. It made him laugh sometimes to see her gazing so quietly and intently at them.

He reached down and massaged her ears, and she purred in response.

KC was a sterling example of a 'tuxedo cat.' She was beautiful with bright green eyes and jet-black fur over most of her feline body. Her short black fur contrasted with her pure white socks and an upside down triangle-shaped patch of white fur under her neck. Her face was small and covered with black fur with long white whiskers growing above her green eyes and on either side of her black nose. Her black and white fur gave her a striking appearance.

Mark reached down and gently rubbed her left ear a moment, and then he rubbed her right ear.

She purred appreciatively.

"Who's my pretty kitty?"

"Meee-owww."

"Look out the window, girl. There's a baby mockingbird hopping around in the yard with Mom nearby."

KC walked over to the base of the window, placed her front paws on the ledge, and gazed out. "Mrrrrr-owww."

"Yes, it's a baby bird."

Mark marveled at the beauty of the little bird -- he had grown into an exact image of an adult, albeit a smaller version, but something seemed different about this mockingbird. Then he realized what it was. This bird had a hurt leg! Yes, that was why it hopped around on one leg; its other leg was obviously hurt and drawn up to its body.

He felt his heart go out to the little fella.

The little bird suddenly went still with his head cocked toward the house. The mockingbird realized he was under observation.

Mark and the baby mockingbird watched each other a moment in mutual awe.

With a flash of wings, the bird flew toward the lower branches of a tall poplar tree near the chain link fence.

Mark chuckled and sat back in his chair.

A hummingbird feeder hung outside the left-most section of the bay window. He had spent many happy moments watching the tiny birds feeding voraciously from it and jealously guarding it from all other hummingbirds. This summer he had one male and he suspected no less than three females feeding regularly at it, though one of the small females might be a hatching year male -- not yet mature enough to sport the iridescent red gorget on his throat that gave this species its common name: ruby-throated hummingbird.

Here at the table with his binoculars at hand, he could also see his two bird feeders that were hung farther out in the backyard. One he filled with black sunflower seed, and the other he filled with a mixture of seed. He loved to watch all the different kinds of birds who visited them on a regular basis. Sometimes he was treated by the sight of a rare, shy bird such as an indigo bunting. Catching a glimpse of one of those blue jewels made his entire week!

Other small creatures also came into view at times. Sometimes a tiny chipmunk would scurry around and gather up seed on the ground to take back to his nest in the small stand of woods next to his house. A colony of green lizards lived in the bushes around his house, and Mark often observed them sunning themselves and running about. Many colorful kinds of butterflies danced through the air as they visited the flowers and flowering bushes around his yard.

And of course, there were the ubiquitous squirrels.

They aggravated Mark to no end, always stealing seed meant for his birds. Mark and the tree-rats were lifelong enemies, sworn to fight an eternal war, though it seemed the squirrels always won out in the end, no matter what trick Mark tried in order to protect his bird feeders.

He heard rapid-fire squeaking that meant a hummingbird was nearby. He looked up with anticipation and spotted a beautiful male hovering just outside the window and peering inside at him.

"Honey!"

Mark remained silent, watching the sunlight sparkle off the iridescent green feathers on the hummer's back as he continued to hover. Suddenly, he rose straight up a few inches and then turned, the sunlight catching the ruby red feathers of his neck and causing them to sparkle like jewels.

"Honey, where are you?"

The hummingbird shot away in a flash of color.

Mark turned as his wife walked in the kitchen door.

"There you are -- why didn't you answer me?"

Jane asked with a hint of exasperation.

"I was watching a hummingbird. He just flew off." Mark smiled apologetically.

"I'm ready to go on my walk. Do you and the kids want to join me?"

"Yes, my dearest Jane Wentworth," Mark said in a comical British accent. "I'd love to accompany you on a stroll through the neighborhood. Let me get Master Philip and Mistress Kate. They also require their daily constitutional, I do believe."

Mark and Jane laughed at his antics while he rose to get the children.

A few minutes later, the Wentworth family walked outside as the summer day slowly turned to dusk. Mark's wife walked every day for exercise, but during the summer she preferred to wait until the heat of the day had waned with the setting sun before going out. On the weekends, Mark and the kids would join her, though they did it as much for the association as the exercise.

Mark brought his small binoculars along in case he spotted any interesting birds.

The family of four walked steadily down Willow Hollow as the shadows lengthened. Jane walked a bit faster than the others since her primary motive was exercise. Mark and the two small children ambled along a few steps behind her. If Jane got too far ahead, Mark called out and she would circle back to them and slow her pace in order to share bits of conversation.

At times, the parents would ask the children how their day had gone. At other times, the parents would talk to each other while the children frolicked around them in made-up dances and other games which small children love. And sometimes, they all walked in comfortable silence and simply enjoyed being together.

People driving by waved at them, and all four of them waved back in a friendly way.

As they turned down another street, a flash of blue caught Mark's eye. He stopped and peered up at the wires between the telephone poles. Jane continued on, unaware that Mark and the kids had stopped.

"What is it, Dad?" Katie asked, gazing in the same direction.

"Bluebirds. I see a mom and a dad and two babies on that telephone wire over there."

"I can't see them," Philip whimpered.

Mark squatted down until he was level with Philip and then pointed up at the four birds.

"Oh! I see them!" Philip said excitedly.

"How do you know one is the wife and one the husband?" Katie asked.

"The male bluebird has electric blue feathers, all over his back and tail. He has a red breast and white belly. See him over there."

"Yes!" the two said together as the bird suddenly flew off.

"The female has bluish-brown feathers on her back, but she has the same red breast feathers. The immature babies resemble the mother when they're young. It's usually the next year after they hatch that the male gets his beautiful sky-blue feathers."

"Dad, you know everything about birds, don't you!" Philip said with childish awe.

"Well, I know a few things about them." Mark tousled Philip's hair.

"Why don't the bluebirds come to your feeders, Dad?" Katie crossed her arms.

"Bluebirds eat insects. See, the male just flew off so he can catch insects in the air right now. If we watch a bit longer, the female will take off and catch some bugs of her own."

"Ewwwwww," Philip said, scrunching his face into a scowl. "They eat bugs!"

"Well, that's what they like."

"Look, Mom's way down there." Philip pointed at his mom's figure far ahead.

"Jane!" Mark called out. "Circle back for us."

Jane dutifully turned. Her bright, laughing smile beamed at them even though she was almost a hundred feet away.

"What are you guys stopped for?" she called out.

"Bluebirds!" Mark replied, pointing up at the wires.

At just that moment, the female and both babies took flight. Mark and the kids watched a moment while the birds dove and swooped after bugs flying in the evening light.

Their heads turned in unison as a bird sang out a wonderful, vibrant song.

"I don't see it," Philip said with frustration as he looked all around.

It took Mark a few moments to spot the bird as

113

well. Each time the bird sang out its joyful song, he followed the sound until he saw the bird perched in the topmost branch of a tree.

"There, kids. All the way at the top of that tree."

The mockingbird's long tail drooped down as it raised its head high and opened its beak. Singing out with all its heart, the bird cocked its tail up and down with its earnest efforts.

"He's a *singer*."

"What's a singer?" Katie asked with a puzzled expression.

Mark smiled. "Well, that's what I call them." He squatted on the ground to be at eye level with the kids. "A 'singer' is a bird who is so happy, he wants everyone to hear him. Like that bird up there, a singer will find the highest point around, whether it's the highest branch in the tallest tree, or the roof of a building or the top of a telephone pole. Then the bird will sing his heart out, serenading the world with his joyful song. I've heard some birds sing for an hour or more. One summer, we had a mockingbird sing for hours on end. Your mom and I could hear him even inside the house. He'd even sing long into the night while we lay in bed."

"Are mockingbirds the only singers?" Katie peered hard into her dad's eyes.

"No, I've seen robins and cardinals sing like that. The other morning, I saw a towhee sitting in the top of one of our trees singing toward the rising sun. Last month, as I left for work, I noticed a song sparrow singing away in the top of a magnolia tree.

I noticed him in the same tree and even the same branch several mornings in a row just singing away." Mark shook his head and smiled. "That was one happy bird."

"What makes them so happy?" Philip put his little arm on his dad's shoulder and leaned on him.

"I guess the same things that make us happy. A beautiful sunrise or his friends... or maybe..." Mark laughed mischievously as he paused.

"What, Dad?" Katie and Philip squealed together, anticipating their dad saying something silly.

"Maybe he had so much fun flying around in the sky he felt he had to sing about it and let us all know!"

"I like that reason," Philip said.

"Ya'll come on -- I need to walk another thirty minutes." Jane had almost reached them when she turned around and started walking away from them again.

"Let's go, kids." Mark took Philip and Katie by the hands, and they hurried to catch up.

They walked around the peaceful neighborhood and finally made their way back home as the sun set below the tree line on the western horizon.

As the children ran upstairs to their respective rooms, Jane and Mark walked into the den. Mark sat down in his easy chair while Jane sat down on the leather couch.

They sat there in mutual silence for several minutes while Mark read the paper and Jane flipped through a magazine she picked up from the coffee table. After a few minutes, she looked up.

"Mark, do you remember Cathy Lewis?"

"Mmmm," Mark said with a non-committal tone.

"Honey, did you hear me?"

Mark looked up from his paper. "I'm sorry, did you say something?"

Jane gave him one of her patented looks of frustration. "Don't you listen to me when I talk to you?"

"I'm sorry, baby, but you saw I was reading."

She looked back at her magazine, but she continued speaking. "Anyway, I ran into Cathy yesterday. You remember, she works at the regional hospital."

"Oh yes, I remember meeting her. She lives over on Greenbrook Court, right?"

"Yes, three streets over from us."

"Everything fine with her and her family?" Mark asked as he glanced back at his newspaper with a hopeful expression.

"Well, she said something that kind of scared me."

Mark set the newspaper down on his lap with a rustle. "What do you mean?"

"She told me the doctors have reported a significant increase in women miscarrying in our county." She looked at her husband with a worried expression. "In fact, the rate is almost twenty times the national average."

"Wow, that's bad."

"And she told me something even worse. She

116

said a large number of the women who lost their babies live in this part of the county -- several lived right in our neighborhood!"

"You're kidding!"

"Mark, I'm scared. What could it be?"

"Could be something they ate. Or, maybe they'll pin it down to some medication they were all taking. Remember the fifties and the Thalidomide babies."

Jane shuddered. "That was horrible -- I've seen pictures of those poor babies."

"Or maybe some kind of pollution in the air," Mark suggested.

"There aren't any factories on this side of Atlanta," Jane said after a moment in thought. "And doesn't the state and federal government regulate output from factories?"

"That's true. There haven't been any accidental releases since that explosion at a chemical warehouse over in Conyers a few years back."

"What could be causing the deaths of these unborn babies?" Jane's expression grew fearful and sad.

"I don't know." Mark shrugged. "Maybe something in the water?"

"That's so scary. Everyone drinks water, and if it's tainted..." Jane's eyes widened.

"Maybe there are only trace amounts of some kind of pollution in the water, a chemical or something just strong enough so that it only affects unborn babies."

"Oh, Mark! How many times have we read

about recalls on food because they're tainted with something, and people have died from eating it before the government warned us. Could we be eating or drinking something harmful to us right this very minute? And weeks or months later the experts will discover it and warn everyone... *but it could be too late for some of us.*" Jane shook her head with an expression of deep worry in her eyes.

"Honey, water is tested all the time; there are strict regulations on that, and I'm pretty sure the air is tested regularly, especially around a major city like Atlanta. We know food is tested, and medicines go through rigorous testing before they're allowed to be used by the public."

A forlorn sigh escaped from Jane. "But we still hear of people dying or getting sick after the fact. Maybe the testing is flawed? Or maybe something new could be out there and they're not even testing for it yet!"

Mark and Jane stared at each for a long moment.

"It's a sad state that man ruins the Earth in so many ways," Mark replied. "And it's not the greed factor that scares me -- it's the accidental or unforeseen side-effects that really scare me."

Jane sat the magazine down and shook her head.

"What are the doctors going to do next?" Mark asked.

"The doctors are preparing a report for the city. I think they're going to submit it to some kind of medical board as well."

"Probably should go to the state too. Maybe even the EPA, if they feel it's something in the environment causing it."

"It's just so scary. I mean, something is causing unborn babies to die -- and no one has any clue. She also said they suspect we are experiencing a higher rate of babies born with deformities, but they still have to gather more information in order to confirm it."

"That means whatever is causing this problem, whether poison or pollution, is affecting the development of babies. It either causes women to miscarry or causes some babies to be malformed."

"Can it hurt our children?"

Mark and Jane looked at each other deeply.

"We'll have to keep track of this situation and what the different agencies discover and report. I assume they'll bring in experts to sample the air and the water and everything else around here to an even greater degree."

"It's not even public. I mean, if I didn't know Cathy, we wouldn't know."

"It'll go public once they send their reports out, and if not, we need to urge them to make it public. Everyone has a right to know something like this is going on around them."

Jane lowered her head as she put her hands to her face.

"You're not crying, are you?" Mark asked.

"Should we move? I mean, if there's something killing babies, it may get bad enough to hurt us, or hurt our children."

"If it is something in the water or in the air, it should affect the animals as much as humans. I haven't heard of anyone reporting any deformities in animals or a high rate of stillborn animals. I think amphibians are most sensitive to pollution in their local environment, and there have been no reports of deformed frogs around here."

"How can we find out if it's affecting the animals? Who checks stuff like that?" Jane asked.

"I don't know. I can search the Internet and see if there is someone or some local department I can contact."

"Didn't DDT kill birds many years ago?"

"Yes, it destroyed their eggs."

"Have you noticed a lot of unhatched eggs when you're bird-watching?"

"Not that I can recall."

"Have you seen any deformed birds?"

"I saw a baby bird with a hurt leg today, but other than that, nothing…"

***

Our Feathered Friends of the Southeast
A. C. Wages

Eastern Bluebird
Latin: *Sialia sialis*

(excerpt)

The Eastern Bluebird is an exceptionally beautiful bird; in males, bright blue feathers cover the back, wings, and tail and contrast with red-orange feathers on the throat, breast, and sides while white feathers cover its belly. The female is similar in coloration with the exception that she wears dull brownish-blue feathers instead of the pure sky-blue of the male. A member of the thrush family, the Eastern Bluebird has a short, slender beak and short legs.

A male bluebird will attract a female by perching above his nest cavity and waving his wings. He will also bring nest material and leave it near the nest cavity, and he will go so far as to hop in and out of the nest cavity in a 'display' for a prospective mate. However, once he finds a mate he has nothing else to do with nest building. The female alone will build the nest and incubate their eggs.

Found exclusively in the Western Hemisphere, the Eastern Bluebird lives year-round throughout the southern section of the United States as well as the island of Bermuda.

Early English settlers of the Virginia colony called it the 'Blue Robin' due to its cheerful song, which reminded them of the English Robin Redbreast back home.

Many Native American tribes revered the bluebird as sacred.

Bluebirds are mentioned in mythology by many indigenous cultures around the world and are associated with the desirable traits of cheerfulness, happiness, and joy. In fact, the mythical 'bluebird' is one of the most commonly accepted symbols of happiness in the entire world. It is from these bluebirds of myth that the real bluebird has attained its association with these same joyous qualities.

The phrase "bluebird of happiness" was used in the play entitled *The Blue Bird* written by the Belgian dramatist and poet Maurice Maeterlinck in 1908. A hit song entitled "The Bluebird of Happiness" was recorded by the famed tenor Jan Peerce in 1934.

The bluebird is the official state bird of two states: Missouri and New York.

The bluebird nests in the cavities of trees much like a woodpecker. In past years, this bird lived primarily in fields and meadows, but it has adapted with the growth of civilization and now dwells in the yards and playgrounds of suburbia.

Bluebird populations have declined with the introduction of the Common Starling and House Sparrow from Europe. These interlopers not only steal their nests but will kill bluebirds if they find them inside the nest cavity.

This beautiful bird is in need of our help -- putting up a bluebird house approximately five to six feet off the ground will discourage the House Sparrow from seeking such a low nesting site while providing the bluebird an optimum nesting site near your home.

NOTE: Choose a metal pole to mount the bluebird house in order to prevent cats or other animals climbing and disturbing the nest. Also, if you decide to build a bluebird house, consult with a reputable source on both materials and how to build it in such a way to attract these beautiful birds and provide them a home near you.

In return, you'll discover that the bluebird really does bring you a little bit of happiness.

Chapter Eleven

Bluesky loved to fly.

Bluesky soon discovered he could fly even higher and faster when a fresh breeze blew, although he was still a little afraid to fly too high. In fact, as he flew near the topmost branches of the trees, a sudden feeling of apprehension filled his heart and he avoided flying up into the sky. He didn't feel ready for that experience quite yet.

His confidence grew every day along with his newfound skill.

Bluesky's days were filled with family as he flexed his wings. He and his siblings never strayed far from Mom and Dad the first full week after they left the nest.

Treetop and Sunshine continued to diligently feed their babies, but now the babies watched in keen fascination as their parents stalked and snagged bugs with the expertise gained through experience. The babies soon realized a change had come in their relationship with their parents.

After they observed a successful hunt by one of their parents, each baby would still fly over and vigorously flap their wings with beak wide open, begging for a morsel.

Treetop and Sunshine now changed their tactics. As they hunted among the blades of grass, they slowed their efforts.

The effect was two-fold: The babies grew hungrier than they ever had before.   More importantly, after close observance of their parents they realized food was readily available all around them -- if they would only hunt for themselves.

Their innate instinct combined with this realization, multiplied by their growing hunger, grew so powerful that the babies leapt into hunting on their own.

Cloudshadow, Songjoy, and Bluesky grew to understand the meaning of the second greatest bird proverb -- '*Bugs are everywhere.*'

Bluesky found it difficult at first. It seemed that every time he spotted a bug crawling on a blade of grass, right as he stabbed at it with his curved, slender beak, the silly thing jumped away.

He grew quite frustrated after his first attempts were unsuccessful and his hunger continued unfulfilled. But suddenly a particularly large and juicy-looking bug crawled into sight.

Bluesky's hunting instinct filled his being as he cocked his head to one side in order to target his victim. He steeled his body and slowly lowered his head in preparation for his attack. Inside his heart, Bluesky knew he was going to catch this bug -- it was crawling so slowly and it was so much bigger than the others he had missed.

He crouched lower, ready to pounce and relieve the burning hunger that filled his belly. He opened his beak slightly as he readied himself. His target moved slowly and awkwardly from one blade of grass to another. As it crossed over a third blade, it seemed to lose its balance...

Bluesky stabbed with his beak.

But just in the nick of time, the bug spread its wings and flew away.

"Ahhhhh!" Bluesky whistled in frustration.

"Now, now, you did much better that time," Treetop said.

"But, it got away, and I'm hungry!"

"Right before you attack, you need to distract it. Remember, if you can see the bug, it can see you too."

"What do you mean?" Bluesky hopped closer.

"That's why, right before I'm ready to strike, I spread my wings. It startles the bugs into flight. I see what direction they're taking, and then I snatch them with my beak."

"Oh…"

"Try again, son."

Bluesky hopped around a few minutes, and soon another bug came into view. He peered intently while he slowly hopped closer. Right as he got within striking range, both he and the bug froze. Bluesky and the bug stared at each other, as if daring the other to make the first move.

He felt an overwhelming urge to strike and feed his hunger immediately, but as the bug sat frozen under his stare, he remembered his father's words.

Bluesky opened his wings.

The reaction was immediate; the bug opened its wings and started to fly off to Bluesky's right. Bluesky stabbed with his beak and felt the crunch as he nabbed his prey, and with a few quick bites, he swallowed it with keen satisfaction.

"I did it! I did it!" he chirped happily.

"Yes, a real milestone -- *your first bug*. I'm so happy for you!" Sunshine flew low over the grass and landed right beside him.

Bluesky felt a deep satisfaction inside his heart, a burning sense of accomplishment. He realized he had fed himself for the first time, and he realized he had taken a major step in growing to adulthood.

Of course, he had also seen his mom catch a bug right before his successful catch. He opened his beak almost without realizing it.

"Feed me! Feed me!" he cried.

Sunshine fed him without hesitation. They were both so used to the process. Still, they both knew Bluesky was fast approaching a new stage of life. Bluesky would now begin to feed himself more and more as his parents began to hunt to feed themselves alone, ignoring the intermittent cries from their babies.

As the sun sank lower in the sky, all three babies grew more adept at capturing their prey with each new attempt.

With the exception of Bluesky, who hopped cautiously on one leg in the grass, the mockingbirds walked stealthily as they hunted for more bugs.

The shadows grew longer. Bluesky missed several more bugs, each one just slightly faster than himself as it flew off, but now, as he stood still and looked around, a bug crawled into view right before him.

His eyes widened with surprise at this unexpected gift. He felt a thrill inside his heart as the feeling of victory filled his being. It seemed there was no way this bug could escape.

He drew his head back with beak open and suddenly struck out at his unwary prey, but somehow, everything went wrong all at once.

In his overwhelming urge to strike, his body moved so forcefully that he lost his balance. As he tried to guide his beak he realized he was falling forward and to one side. Bluesky extended his wings in a vain attempt to regain his delicate balance.

This was always a challenge for him and always would be. A single leg held all his weight, but Bluesky had realized even way back in the nest that he had to hold his body slightly to the side in order to center his weight on it.

After he left the nest, new challenges arose. He found that after any movement, and especially any sudden movements, if he leaned too far to the left he would always lose his balance and fall. Because of this, he had to consciously will himself to hold his body at an angle.

Bluesky usually squatted low to the ground when he paused. This helped take the stress off his leg. When he stood upright and held his body at an angle, it placed a constant strain on his hip joint -- and he felt a constant ache that always reminded him he only had one leg.

The more he hopped and moved around the more he realized that the window where he could hold his body 'in balance' was small, and he had to constantly correct himself by fluttering his wings. To onlookers he seemed like an extremely nervous bird, as if he were constantly in fear and ready to fly away, but once his missing leg was seen, his constant fluttering seemed to magnify his pitiable condition.

Now with his forceful strike, he had not only lost his balance, but he'd also overcompensated in his urge to continue the attack. With a frantic flurry of wings, Bluesky fell flat on his face.

While he lay there a moment, he heard the tinkling laughter of Cloudshadow and Songjoy

His face grew hot with embarrassment as he struggled to stand.

"That was hilarious, I've never seen a bird flap his wings so hard and not take off!" Cloudshadow laughed out loud.

Even worse, Bluesky now watched as the bug zoomed lazily away. He struggled to rise and somehow fell right back down with his beak in the dirt.

"Bluesky, that was funny! Do it again!" Songjoy added with a laughing chirp, but it didn't feel funny at all to him. In fact, it made him feel sad and even angry.

"Come on, babies," Sunshine said with a comforting tone. "Bluesky is learning, and I'd like to see either of you catch a bug using just one leg."

"I can do it," Cloudshadow said confidently. "Just watch."

Cloudshadow raised one leg and hopped forward. He lost his balance immediately as he flapped his wings, but right before he lost his balance completely and fell, he lowered his other leg.

"See, it's not that easy," Sunshine said.

"Well, he still looked funny falling right on his face," Cloudshadow replied with a hurt expression.

"It was funny," Songjoy added with a chirp.

"I didn't think it was funny," Bluesky said sulkily.

He felt his embarrassment burning across his face. He didn't like falling, and he didn't like his brother and sister laughing at him.

He keenly felt his disadvantage. Not for the first time he wondered why he had been born with just one leg while Cloudshadow and Songjoy had been born with two -- like normal birds.

"That's enough from you two." Treetop raised his voice with a stern, warning tone.

Cloudshadow and Songjoy returned to hunting, but Bluesky lowered his head as he stood silently.

"Bluesky, don't let their laughter get you down," Sunshine said comfortingly.

"Mama, I'm different than they are, and I fall a lot. They hardly ever fall." Bluesky hung his head sadly.

"They didn't mean anything by it."

"But they laughed at me."

"Have they done anything that made you laugh at them?" Sunshine asked.

Bluesky thought a moment. "I laughed when Cloudshadow missed that bug a while back and then kept hopping and flapping after it as it flew around and around him." Bluesky opened his beak in a smile.

"I laughed too, and he never got it, did he? In spite of all that flapping and jumping around!" Sunshine chuckled softly.

Bluesky laughed along with her a moment at the funny memory, but remembering his embarrassment, he lowered his head again.

"We all do funny things sometimes, Bluesky, and birds may laugh at us, but as long they don't do it in a mean or spiteful way, don't take it badly."

Bluesky continued to stare at the ground.

"We have to be able to laugh at ourselves. We can't be too sensitive, baby." Sunshine brushed her feathers against Bluesky in a comforting way. "If we're too sensitive, birds won't know how to act around us, and then they'll shy away from being your friend."

Bluesky perked up at his mother's words and her touch.

"When will we meet other birds?" Bluesky chirped with excitement. "I'd like to meet other birds my age and play with them."

"Don't you like playing with your brother and sister?" Sunshine asked with a hint of humor, knowing what his answer would be.

"Yes, I like flying and playing chase with them, but I'd like to play with somebody new."

Sunshine smiled at her baby.

"All birds start out by staying close with their family, but as you grow and fly farther and farther away each day, you will meet other birds…"

Chapter Twelve

Bluesky perched on a branch high in a pine tree and chirped happily. His song was a simple imitation of his parents' favorite song. He sang it with pride and whistled the notes to the best of his ability.

He froze in surprise when he suddenly heard the same song repeated back to him exactly as he'd sung it. He cocked his tail excitedly and hopped farther out on the branch, peering intently in the direction of the unseen singer.

It sounded as if the song had come from the next tree over, but he couldn't see the bird among the thick foliage.

"Was that you, Cloudshadow?" Bluesky called out.

"Not me!" Cloudshadow flew down from a branch just above him and landed beside Bluesky. "Was it Songjoy?" Cloudshadow asked as he and Bluesky peered over at the other tree.

"No, I'm down here eating." Songjoy looked up at them from the grass below, munching appreciatively on an especially crunchy bug.

Cloudshadow and Bluesky stared over at the other tree in puzzlement.

The unseen singer sang out again in perfect imitation of Bluesky's song.

"He's playing with you," Cloudshadow said without hesitation.

"W-what should I do?" Bluesky asked, looking

to his older sibling for guidance.

"It's a challenge! He's playing the 'Singing Game' with you. Sing back, but louder and stronger."

Bluesky hopped excitedly about a few moments, readying himself for the game. He fluffed out his feathers proudly, now realizing this other bird was trying to out-sing him, but Bluesky was going to show him.

Holding his wings tight against his sides, he raised his head and sang out with every ounce of energy and with every fiber of his being. As he sang the last note, he cocked his head to one side and waited expectantly.

After a few seconds, the unseen bird repeated his song, cheerfully and effortlessly and note for note. Right at the end, however, he added a flurry of extra chirps and whistles.

"Sing it back to him, exactly as he did!" Cloudshadow jumped up and down on the branch with excitement. "And add that last bit just like he did, but sing it better!"

Bluesky felt the excitement too. Again, he threw his head back and sang out loudly, adding the new part exactly as the other bird had sung it.

Even as he whistled the last note, the other bird repeated the song again.

Cloudshadow and Bluesky looked at each other with a smile.

"Let's go see who this other bird is!" With a flash of feathers, Cloudshadow flew toward the tree.

Bluesky leapt into the air and soared after

Cloudshadow.

Down below, Songjoy had watched and listened to the game with the other unseen bird. When she saw her brothers flying rapidly to the other tree, she flew after them.

Bluesky landed on a branch about mid-way up the tree. He looked around in all directions, first seeking Cloudshadow, who he spotted two branches down. Now, he sought the other bird that had played the song game with him.

"Here I am!" The chirping voice came from above Bluesky. Five branches up, a young mockingbird smiled down at him.

Bluesky flew up and landed right beside him. "What's your name?" Bluesky asked excitedly.

"Funwind!"

"I like your name," Bluesky said. "My name is Bluesky."

"Hi, I'm Cloudshadow." Cloudshadow flew up and perched on the other side of Funwind.

"My name is Songjoy." Songjoy landed beside Bluesky.

All three of them stared at the new bird inquisitively.

He looked just like them, a typical young mockingbird. Still, they were in amazement at meeting their first new friend.

"Catch me if you can!" Funwind leapt into the air between the branches and soared into the open air between the trees.

Bluesky, Cloudshadow, and Songjoy flew after him in the age-old game of 'Fly and Seek.' They followed him as he flew in and around the trees. They saw Funwind look over his shoulder as they gained on him. Suddenly, he folded his wings and dove for the ground. Just when it looked like he would crash, he flapped his wings and soared into a group of nearby bushes.

The trio lost ground on him after Funwind dove, but they beat their wings faster and flew into the bushes in hot pursuit.

Bluesky perched in the shadows right in the middle of the largest bush. He saw Cloudshadow over to his side and Songjoy on the ground. All three of them hopped around, eagerly seeking Funwind's hiding place.

After a few moments, they found themselves perched on the same bush -- but there was still no sign of Funwind. Bluesky looked at Cloudshadow and Songjoy in puzzlement.

"Here I am!" Funwind whistled mischievously. He peered down at them from near the top of a bush several feet away. He laughed at them a moment and then leapt up and flew away again.

"Come on, catch me!" he yelled back at them as he disappeared.

Bluesky was readying himself when he felt a wing on his back.

"Hold on a second," Cloudshadow said. "He's pretty fast. Let's outsmart him."

"Wow, a great idea! What do you have in mind?" Bluesky whistled.

Songjoy hopped closer to hear her older brother's plan.

"You two chase him; I'll fly up high and watch until I see where I can head him off."

"Good plan," Songjoy chirped.

Bluesky and Songjoy leapt together from the bushes and flew after Funwind. A moment later, Cloudshadow took flight, but instead of chasing along with them, he flew higher and higher.

Bluesky saw Funwind fly through the branches of a nearby tree. He turned and soared after him with Songjoy at his wingtip.

Funwind led them on a merry chase. He zoomed in and out of the trees and sometimes over the tops of trees. He flew up and around until suddenly he flew right through the branches and soared up and over and between the myriad of leaves and limbs.

Bluesky and Songjoy gave chase and held their own with Funwind's every move, but as soon as they would gain on him, he would dart away in another direction and put more distance between them.

It seemed they would never catch him.

Suddenly, just as Funwind started to soar around another tree, Cloudshadow dove out of the sun. With a playful peck, he nipped at the feathers on Funwind's back.

"Tag! Got you!" Cloudshadow shouted in triumph.

"Aw, that wasn't fair." Funwind landed on a branch, but his broad smile gave away his true feelings.

"What wasn't fair about it? I caught you, fair

and square." Cloudshadow laughed as he landed on the branch beside Funwind.

Seconds later, Bluesky and Songjoy joined them.

"You weren't chasing me! You were waiting high up in the sky until I came to you!" Funwind complained breathlessly.

"Seems fair to me -- I still caught you." Cloudshadow laughed.

The four birds perched on the branch in order to catch their breath before they started another chase.

After a few moments, three more young mockingbirds joined them.

"This is my sister, Moonnight."

Bluesky and his siblings sang greetings to her.

"And these are my other friends, Eveningbreeze and Daysinger."

The two young male mockingbirds exchanged song greetings with everyone.

"Catch me if you can!" Moonnight shouted as she leapt into the air.

The young mockingbirds played and played, soaring through the air with happy calls and whistles. As soon as one of them 'tagged' the bird being chased, that bird now became the one to catch. They flew at breakneck speed among the tree branches and out into the open air, soaring around the trees and up into the sky above the treetops.

Finally, they all landed in the same tree, each one exhausted and breathless.

Bluesky's heart pounded inside his breast as he landed on a branch next to Daysinger and Songjoy.

The seven mockingbirds, once they got their breath, now chattered and sang to each other, each trying to outdo the other. They imitated each other's songs, and sometimes they imitated the songs of chickadees, titmice, or sparrows who sang nearby.

Finally, satisfied they were each the greatest singer of them all, the mockingbirds settled down and chattered happily among themselves. Their 'song game' had not really been in earnest, as was the way of adult mockingbirds who flew to the highest perch and endeavored to outsing any bird who came near their home territory. No, their song game was really practice for the time they would mark their own territory and protect it and sing for it.

Bluesky marveled at his new friends. He liked them. They were fun to play with, as much fun as Songjoy and Cloudshadow, but after a few moments, he realized they were all staring back at him with puzzled expressions.

"Why don't you put your other leg down, Bluesky?" Eveningbreeze asked with his tail cocked up with interest.

"I only have one leg," Bluesky said with a hint of embarrassment.

"Really!" Funwind said in surprise. "Does it hurt?"

"No." Bluesky looked at him in equal surprise. "Why do you say that?"

"It just seems like it would hurt, when you lost your leg."

"I was born with only one leg."

"Ohhhh," Moonnight crooned.

The new birds all looked at him strangely.

"Hey, let's play 'Fly and Seek again!'" Cloudshadow shouted.

"Wait a second", Funwind scowled.

"What's the matter?" Cloudshadow looked at Funwind with surprise.

"I'm always the one who decides what we do." Funwind looked around with an air of superiority. "You can't just come into our group and take over, you know."

"Can't others decide what we're going to play?" Cloudshadow shrugged with uncertainty.

"Nope."

Bluesky, Songjoy and Cloudshadow looked around at the other birds to see if they agreed.

"Funwind's right," Daysinger said. "He always thinks of the best things to do. We always let him decide."

Funwind smiled confidently. "See, I'm the leader of our group. If you want to play with us, you'll have to listen to me too."

Songjoy rolled her eyes.

Bluesky remained silent, trying to figure out if this was good or not.

"Okay, well, what are we going to do?" Cloudshadow asked.

"Let's see who can fly to the highest branch first!" Funwind chirped excitedly.

"Okay, let's play that." Cloudshadow nodded.

"Let's go!" Funwind shouted in reply.

The seven birds soared up through the tree seeking the topmost branch.

After a few moments, Songjoy perched highest, her body swaying in the wind as the slender limb moved with the summer breeze. The others perched just below her on other branches, and the seven mockingbirds chattered happily among themselves.

But although everyone seemed happy and acted like they were having fun, Bluesky felt the constant gaze of the new birds on his missing leg. Soon, it made him feel uncomfortable.

As the rest sat and sang happily, Funwind flew to sit beside Bluesky. "You look weird."

"No, I don't," Bluesky replied angrily.

"Yes, you do. Actually, you're a strange bird and kind of creepy. Everyone feels the same way I do." Funwind pointed his wings back at Moonnight, Daysinger, and Eveningbreeze.

Bluesky noticed their disapproving stares.

"I have two wings," Bluesky said defensively.

"You look too queer though," Funwind said with an air of superiority. "And we don't want to play with you anymore."

Songjoy swooped down and landed beside Bluesky. "If he can't play, I don't want to play with you either." Songjoy stepped closer to Bluesky.

"Yeah!" Cloudshadow said in agreement. "If he goes, I go."

"Okay, okay," Funwind said with exasperation. "Hey, let's go fly over to that yard over there. The man mowed the grass earlier today, and it's easy to find bugs."

The seven mockingbirds each flew to a separate section and began hunting in earnest, each of them famished from their exertions.

Bluesky hunted diligently, hopping slowly forward and spreading his wings to scare the bugs into movement so he could eat them. He had eaten several when he noticed Funwind talking to some of the others by the bushes at the edge of the yard.

Songjoy and Cloudshadow were not with them; they were hunting bugs off to themselves. Bluesky thought nothing of it and continued eating.

After a few moments, Funwind flew over and landed near him. "Bluesky, I want to say something to you."

Bluesky looked at him questioningly.

"Listen, me and my friends, we don't like you. We think you look *creepy* with only one leg."

"I do not!"

Funwind stared at his missing leg. "Yeah, you look weird, almost like you should fall over any moment."

Sadness spread deeply inside Bluesky's heart.

"But we like your sister and your brother. However, we won't play with them either if you stay. So unless you want us to hurt their feelings, you should fly away. In fact, why don't you fly back to your parents so we can play with them, okay?"

Bluesky looked away as his eyes filled with tears; he couldn't look this bird in the eyes any more. He had liked Funwind -- he'd thought he was a good bird, but now he didn't know what to think.

"Sure, I'll fly back and find Mom and Dad."

He leapt up and flew towards the tree where he had been born. He knew it was the center of his parents' home territory.

He didn't want to play with Funwind and the others anyway.

"Where is Bluesky going?" Songjoy asked as Funwind flew up to her and Cloudshadow.

"He said he missed his parents, and he was tired of playing too. Hey, me and my friends want to show you our secret place. There are three trees that grow together, and the branches are so thick you can't fly through them."

"That sounds like fun," Cloudshadow said.

With a flurry of wings, the six mockingbirds flew off together.

Perched in a tree a short distance away, Bluesky watched the birds fly off with a sadness that filled his soul. He had paused, hoping his siblings might not want to go with the other birds if he wasn't there. But Cloudshadow and Songjoy hadn't even looked for him. They just left with the other birds without a glance. In his heart, he felt his brother and sister preferred the company of these new birds over him now, and that thought made him feel even more sad.

He hung his head and uttered a forlorn whistle. He felt like the loneliest bird in the world.

As the others disappeared into the distant trees, he took flight again, and a short time later he landed in the yard with the dogwood tree that held his birth nest.

He didn't see his parents anywhere, but instead of seeking them out, he decided he would hunt some bugs on his own. After all, he didn't need anyone anyhow.

He hunted around the yard alone for a long time in bitter silence. His thoughts grew troubled, and many times the bugs escaped right underneath his beak.

Bluesky's sadness was soon replaced with frustration. It seemed everything was going wrong for him today.

As he hopped around the blades of grass seeking more bugs, he suddenly heard a bird singing from the thick bushes beside the fence.

Bluesky stood frozen as he listened intently, but the unseen bird in the bushes did not repeat its warbling snippet of song.

This confused Bluesky, for the bird's song resembled a mockingbird's, but mockingbirds usually repeated their favorite phrases two or more times. In fact, Bluesky already instinctively knew that when a mockingbird became enthralled with a new song or a new melody he felt compelled to sing that same song over and over until his passion for it was satisfied.

Bluesky already felt the strong stirrings that inspired all mockingbirds. Deep inside, his emotions boiled like a volcano at hearing this new song. The burning urge to reply like a true songster filled his being.

As this feeling of inner exhilaration pounded inside his heart, he realized why his kind were apt to break forth in song at any moment.

Their great passion was what made mockingbirds renowned throughout the world as the greatest singers, but it also made mockingbirds extremely jealous.

Jealousy was not a good trait among birds, but this extreme jealously was one reason why mockingbirds would mimic the song of any bird they hear. Mockingbirds instinctively felt they must prove to every bird that they alone among all the birds were the supreme singers.

This was the reason that after the game of 'Fly and Seek', the most popular game among young mockingbirds is the 'Singing Game' -- a duel to outsing the other bird. This game alone was played by mockingbirds their entire lives as they endeavored to outsing any bird who dared to sing within earshot.

Bluesky waited with a bit of puzzlement.

Finally, the unseen bird sang the warbling snippet of song again.

As the last note floated in the air, the bird once again did not repeat it.

Bluesky heard in the bird's voice that it was a young bird like himself, and like any decent mockingbird, Bluesky felt he must repeat the song of this other bird and sing it louder and better!

Stretching his wings apart, Bluesky looked upward and sang the song note for note, but like a good mockingbird, Bluesky repeated the song three times. When he finished, he cocked his tail expectantly and peered into the shadows of the bush as if daring the unseen bird to outdo his performance.

Silence answered.

Bluesky's puzzlement deepened. Perhaps this mockingbird was smarter than the others and dared not sing again in the presence of such a grand singer as himself?

Bluesky smiled.

Suddenly, that unseen singer sang his song again -- with no repeats. The bird sang each note in exactly the fashion Bluesky first heard it.

"Ah, so you want to play the 'Singing Game' with me!" Bluesky cried out.

Bluesky hopped closer to the bush in order to get a look at this bird that refused to repeat its song.

Suddenly, a strange sound came to Bluesky's ears.

"Mew."

The bird's tone had changed. This single phrase was uttered with a fussing, chattering cry.

It made Bluesky's heart jump with fear, although he wasn't quite sure why. He stared in silence at the moving shadows beneath the thick stand of bushes.

"Well," Bluesky chirped. "I've never heard a bird make a sound like that before!"

Only silence answered, which made Bluesky all the more nervous. He felt a strong urge to hop into the bushes and meet this new bird. On the other hand, he was afraid to go any closer -- he couldn't make out anything within the deep shadows.

His parents' words echoed in his mind,

important lessons they had repeated over and over to him: *Be careful whenever you are on the ground. Look and listen. Always be aware of everything around you -- because there are animals about that love nothing better than to catch a bird!*

Bluesky shivered. "Hello, is there a bird in there?" he asked cautiously.

"Meeeewwwww."

It has to be a bird. I heard its song just a moment ago.

He hopped until he reached the edge of the shadows and peered inside.

"Mewwww!"

"What kind of bird are you? I've never heard a mockingbird call out like that!"

"Meeeewwww!"

Bluesky's heart beat faster and faster as he tried to get a glimpse of the bird somewhere in the shadows under the bush. But he paused, afraid to go any closer to the frightening shadows. A flurry of emotions boiled inside his feathered breast, but at the same time an overwhelming fear gripped his heart.

He shook himself to get his courage back up. With renewed determination, Bluesky sang the bird's original song in exact imitation and waited for the bird to sing back.

"Mewwwww!" The unseen bird fussed back at him.

Shaking his head with wonder, Bluesky decided this unseen bird must have changed the game. Instead of a song, this bird wanted him to imitate this strange call. Well, he could do that easy.

"Mewwww!" Bluesky repeated exactly.

"Mewwww!" the other cried in an even more fussy tone.

"That's it -- I'm coming in to see who you are," Bluesky whistled, and with a couple of bounding hops, he leapt into the thickest part of the bushes.

Bluesky froze as the deep shadows completely enveloped him.

While his eyes adjusted to the low light, he peered at a sudden movement before him. The lower branches of the bush swayed with movement of the still unseen creature.

He closed his eyelids, forcing his eyes to adjust to the shadows faster. After all, he didn't want the bird to jump out at him and startle him, which might be quite embarrassing..

The lowest branches moved again, but Bluesky could now make out more details -- though he still couldn't see the bird anywhere.

Suddenly, there it was!

He stared in fascination at the bird crouched on the lowest branches. Small streams of light filtered in just enough to break up the deep shadows.

The bird's body was shaped like a mockingbird -- lithe with a long tail and a sharp, down-curved beak -- but this bird had dark gray feathers all over its svelte body, and its wings were edged in black feathers, as was its tail. Right on the tip-top of its head, it sported a small black cap.

"What kind of bird are you?" Bluesky asked in amazement.

"I'm a catbird. I'm your cousin!" the bird replied with a smile.

"What's your name?"

"Shadowflier." In response to its name, the young catbird jumped from one branch to another.

"My name is Bluesky."

"I like that name," Shadowflier chirped excitedly.

"You say we're cousins?" Bluesky asked hesitantly.

"Yes, catbirds are the little cousins to mockingbirds. Brown Thrashers are our big cousins."

"Oh," Bluesky said with a hint of uncertainty.

"Haven't your mother and father taught you about the different families of birds yet?"

"Um, not really.

"I hatched soon after the last frost. When did you hatch?"

"Just over one full moon ago. This is my second full moon now."

"I see. You're younger than I am. Yes, your parents will soon begin teaching you the deeper things about birds." Shadowflier flitted over to a lower branch, and with a burst of energy he hopped onto the ground beside Bluesky.

Bluesky eyed his cousin carefully.

"You're small for a mockingbird," Shadowflier said.

"You're the same size as me," Bluesky said with a defensive tone.

"Catbirds are the smallest of our *family of birds*,

but you're the same size as me."

"Maybe I'll grow some more," Bluesky retorted.

The catbird hopped completely around Bluesky, looking him over. As he hopped around, Bluesky watched him just as carefully.

Bluesky steeled himself. He knew that as soon as the bird realized he only had one leg, he would make fun of him just like Funwind and the other birds had.

Bluesky felt his sadness return, but he didn't realize that the shadows partially hid him.

Shadowflier hopped faster. As the catbird flitted around with boundless energy, he raised his long tail higher until Bluesky caught a flash of red.

"You have red feathers underneath your tail!" Bluesky snickered.

"What's so funny about that?"

"You've got red feathers on your rump!"

"You're just jealous that we catbirds have a wee bit more color than you mockingbirds, cuz."

Bluesky continued chuckling.

"Shadowflier!"

Shadowflier and Bluesky turned toward the new voice.

"That's my mom; I've got to go now."

"Do you live here in the bushes?"

"Yes, catbirds love bushes. There's lots of bugs here, and it's easy to hide and build nests."

"Maybe I'll see you again soon? My birth nest is in that tree over there. My family lives here too -- just not in the bushes."

"You know what they say?" Shadowflier asked.

Bluesky shook his head. "No, what do they say?"

"*Birds of a feather flock together*."

"Oh." Bluesky puzzled over this new bit of bird wisdom he'd never heard before, but just as Shadowflier was about to fly off into the deepest shadows, Bluesky spoke again. "If we're cousins, we're sort the same feather..."

"I don't know, I don't think catbirds and mockingbirds hang out together much."

"Why not?" Bluesky asked.

"I think birds are supposed to only make friends with their own kind." Shadowflier shrugged.

"If we like each other, why can't we be friends?"

"Birds of a feather flock together. I think it's some kind of rule," he repeated.

"It's a dumb rule," Bluesky said with a hint of sadness.

The gray catbird paused with a questioning expression on his face.

"Shadowflier, come here right now, young bird!" his mom called again with a more commanding tone.

Shadowflier looked over his shoulder and smiled as he spread his wings. "Nice meeting you, cuz. Too bad you're not a catbird, then we could be friends."

Chapter Thirteen

Bluesky told his parents and siblings all about the catbird he'd met in the bushes as they perched high in a tree.

"Sunshine!" Treetop gasped. "We've been so busy we've completely forgotten to tell these babies about the 'Families of Birds' and the 'Ways of Birds.'"

Sunshine laughed out loud a moment before speaking. "I guess there was too much to worry about at first. I must admit, I've been plain worn out simply feeding this group of babies, but you're right. We need to teach them what birds are all about."

As the stars appeared in the sky and the full moon rose higher, Bluesky, Songjoy, and Cloudshadow listened intently as their parents told them for the first time about the various families of birds.

Treetop and Sunshine told them about the mimic thrushes first, the family of birds in which they belonged.

They explained that thrashers were famous singers and mimics in their own right. Thrashers mimicked the songs of other birds with a flair almost equal to mockingbirds. Unlike a mockingbird, however, Brown Thrashers sang each phrase of their song only twice, and catbirds rarely, if ever, repeated any phrase of their songs.

But true to their namesakes, thrashers,

151

mockingbirds, and catbirds joyfully and mischievously mimicked the song of any bird that crossed their paths -- or better yet, dared to sing within earshot.

The three babies shivered when they learned about the families of hawks and falcons.

For the first time, they learned that some birds actually hunted and ate other birds -- a frightening thought indeed. Treetop and Sunshine explained that key physical traits among those birds of prey were their powerful talons and large, muscular wings that allowed them to sweep silently and quickly upon unsuspecting birds and small animals.

Bluesky drew back in fear as he heard how hawks would sit silently in trees until an unsuspecting bird flew near them and, without a sound, swoop down and take the poor bird in its powerful talons and kill it.

Thankfully, the other families of birds were less scary.

While the stars multiplied in the darkening sky, they heard about the family of sparrows -- little brown birds who lived in every part of the world. They heard of the different families of thrushes, larks, finches, warblers, egrets, herons, flycatchers, weaverbirds, and countless others. Of course, his parents only hit the high points of each family as a way of introduction.

The babies listened with intense interest as their parents turned to the birds of the sea. They heard for the first time about the raucous seagulls who lived on every shore and flew far out over the sea.

They learned how those birds flocked together in great, seething masses to nest on remote spots to raise their young and also how they shouted, cried, and fought for scraps from the boats of men returning with the day's catch of fish.

Songjoy laughed when they heard about the exotic parrots and macaws who lived in tropical jungles. Treetop and Sunshine laughed themselves as they explained about the roguish exploits of these colorful birds in the jungles and how they even outsmarted humans at times.

And all of them wished they could see a toucan, a black bird whose huge striped beak was almost as big as his entire body.

"Wow! How can a toucan fly?" Cloudshadow exclaimed.

"It must fly with its beak pointed down all the time. I imagine it must be heavy," Songjoy whispered with a far-off look in her eyes.

"Maybe it can't fly and simply walks everywhere?" Bluesky suggested.

"No, a toucan flies as well as any bird," Sunshine chirped happily. "Its beak is not heavy at all."

"Actually, there is a bird with a beak larger than a toucan, and it flies as gracefully as any bird alive," Treetop said with gleaming eyes.

"Really! What bird is that?" Cloudshadow asked excitedly.

"The pelican."

"Where do pelicans live?" Songjoy asked.

"They live on the seashore like seagulls and

terns, the place where the ocean meets the land and the wind always blows, and like the egrets and herons, they eat fish right out of the water, scooping them up with their huge beaks. In fact, the lower half of their beak has a great elastic skin that allows them to scoop up the fish out of the water and hold them until they swallow them whole!"

"Wow!" all three youngsters said together.

"Pelicans have stubby, thick bodies with very short legs. They walk with great difficulty, and look quite awkward on the ground, but..." Sunshine smiled as she noticed the expectant faces waiting for her to finish.

"But once in the air, pelicans fly with their heads held back and their huge beaks pointed straight ahead. They especially love to glide. They will spread their wings and soar just over the tops of the waves. Pelicans love gliding in long lines one after the other. It's kind of a game for them.

"Sometime up to a dozen will fly in single-file formation, gliding for long distances over the waves until the leader spots some fish. The lead pelican will then rise up high into the air as the others follow. At the pinnacle of his climb, the lead pelican will twist his body and point his great beak down at the water, folding his wings up like a hawk and dive straight down into water with a huge splash!"

"I'd love to see a pelican!" Bluesky whistled.

"Maybe you will one day," Sunshine said.

"We have also neglected to tell our babies about the famous Song-Tales," Treetop added with a chuckle. "I guess we've been way too busy feeding and sleeping with this brood."

"Song-Tales?" the three siblings cried out in unison.

"Yes, every family of birds has their own set of Song-Tales -- songs about heroism, love, and friendship. The most famous Song-Tale among mockingbirds is the one about Skysinger."

"What did Skysinger do?" Cloudshadow asked with awe.

"Skysinger was the greatest songster who ever lived among mockingbirds," Sunshine replied. "It was said he could perfectly imitate any song by any bird and on his very first try!"

"The greatest songster of all," Treetop added thoughtfully.

"He could outsing any bird he met, but his great gift for song was also his greatest tragedy." Sunshine looked from one youngster to another.

"What do you mean?" Songjoy finally asked. "Go on, tell us."

"Well, I won't sing his Song-Tale tonight; it's one of the longest tales of all. Suffice it to say that Skysinger had to learn that it's more important to have friends than to be the greatest songster of all. I'll sing it to you one night soon."

"Do all bird families have Song-Tales?" Bluesky hopped closer to his mother and perched right next to her comforting warmth. Cloudshadow and Songjoy perched closer as well as the mockingbird family readied themselves for sleep.

"Yes, some Song-Tales are common among all

birds everywhere in the world. Some Song-Tales were so inspiring that their songs were sung around the world in a single day the first time, chasing the sun around the world until every bird in every tree and in every land both heard and sang it!"

"Awesome!" Cloudshadow chirped.

"Cool!" Songjoy and Bluesky added.

A puzzled expression settled over Songjoy's face as she thought about her mother's last statement. Finally, she gave voice to the question in her heart. "When the birds sing a Song-Tale from another bird family, do they mimic the bird's song like a mockingbird?"

Sunshine laughed. "No. Every bird family has its own dialect, its own peculiar way of singing. What happens is like this -- when a warbler hears a Song-Tale from a flycatcher, the warbler will sing the flycatcher's song in its own dialect, but stay true to the original song of the flycatcher."

"But how can a new Song-Tale go around the world in one day?" Bluesky asked . "I mean, a single day is a short time!"

"And why would a bird want to sing another bird's song?" Cloudshadow added.

"Some Song-Tales are so beautiful, so wonderful, and so moving that any bird who hears it feels compelled to sing it. As you can imagine, very few songs are powerful enough *to move* every bird who hears it to sing it right away, but a few have had such power…"

"But you said Skysinger's Song-Tale was too long to sing tonight. How can such a long song get sung around the world?" Bluesky asked.

"The initial Song-Tale is a concise, little song that conveys the 'heart' of the story."

"It has to be a short song. How else could a bird hear it, remember it, and then sing it in its own dialect and sing it on around the world?" Treetop added.

"And when you hear some of those songs that inspired birds to sing them around the world, you will understand," Sunshine said.

"Which ones?" Songjoy asked excitedly.

"Well, there is the Song-Tale of love between the two nightingales, Merryday and her mate, Eveningsky."

"What's so special about love? Yuck!" Cloudshadow twittered with childish distaste.

"Their love was special. They intended to become lifelong mates, not just mates for a season, like many birds." Sunshine smiled as her eyes focused on something far off in the distance.

"What happened?" the three siblings chirped together.

"Since this Song-Tale is about love between mates, I will sing it to you when you are a little older."

"At least tell us why it's so famous!" Songjoy pleaded.

"Okay, I'll give you the synopsis." Sunshine's eyes grew far off. Finally, she spoke.

"Merryday and Eveningsky met and became lifelong mates in their second season of life, but tragedy unfolded before they even finished their first nest. You see, Eveningsky loved to sing so much that many times he'd sing the entire day. He sang beautifully. In fact, it is said that all the other birds would stop singing and listen when his clear voice rang out through the woods, his songs were so beautiful."

"I bet Merryday loved to sing with him," Songjoy chirped in.

"Yes, I imagine so." Sunshine smiled knowingly at Treetop. Treetop nodded back at her with a gleam in his eyes.

"But it was because of his great gift of song that the tragedy unfolded. A *bird catcher* came to the woods in search of birds to trap and take back to sell for food, but he made more money selling songbirds if he could trap them and cage them for a wealthy client who loved to keep them in wire cages."

"The bird catcher trapped Eveningsky one day after hearing him sing and put him in a cage and sold him to a wealthy merchant who took him to a land far, far away. Eveningsky was heartbroken at being parted from his mate. He was so sad he would now only sing after the sun had set and the night enveloped the world just like the dark sadness that now enveloped his heart, and when he sang, his songs were sad in a beautiful way. He warbled and trilled with a haunting melancholy that filled the night air as he sang of his lost love and how he wished to see her just one more time.

"When the other birds perched for the night and heard his beautiful yet melancholy song about his lost love, they remembered it and sang it themselves in turn the next day in the hope other birds would repeat it until Merryday herself would hear and come to find her mate, and so day after day, week after week, Eveningsky's song for Merryday traveled farther and farther around the world…"

"You said the song went around the world in one day!" Bluesky protested.

"Not Eveningsky's song lamenting his loss of Merryday. The Song-Tale of Merryday and Eveningsky did get sung around the world in a single day -- the day they were finally reunited."

"Keep going!" Songjoy said.

"His song finally reach Merryday, and with the help of a raven, Eveningsky was rescued and both were finally reunited. On that same morning, the Song-Tale of Merryday and Eveningsky was sung out by all the birds who witnessed this joyful event, and every bird who heard that song then sang it on around the world. It is one of the most beautiful songs ever sung."

"Really?" Bluesky asked.

"It was very beautiful, and even today, birds of all families still like to sing their song -- the Song-Tale of Merryday and Eveningsky."

Sunshine looked at her youngsters. "That Song-Tale is one reason why nightingales prefer to sing at night even to this day."

"I want a Song-Tale tonight!" Cloudshadow twittered happily.

"Me too!" Bluesky added enthusiastically.

"Me three!" Songjoy chirped.

"All right. I will sing to you a tale of true

friendship and courage. It is the Song-Tale of Treehopper and his best friend Cloudsky -- two blackpoll warblers."

Sunshine hopped a little farther out on the limb on which they were all perched and fluffed out her feathers as she readied herself for the song. Then, with her head raised high, she sang the original Song-Tale of Treehopper and Cloudsky that was sung around the world. It was a beautiful, lilting melody woven around the tender and courageous story of two young friends.

Cloudshadow, Songjoy, and Bluesky listened as if in a trance.

The simple but powerful song lasted just over two minutes. It quickly grew obvious why this song inspired every bird who heard it to sing it on around the world.

After she finished the Song-Tale, Sunshine then told them the entire, unabridged story…

***

But to know Cloudsky, we must learn something about his particular family of birds.

Blackpoll warblers are small songbirds about the size of sparrows with black caps, white cheeks, and white throats. Their backs are gray with black streaks of feathers. Their wings also are gray with black streaks and two white wing-bars, while their chests are white with thin black streaks.

Blackpolls warblers are famous throughout the world of birds, but not for their singing ability nor for their size or color. These tiny birds are famous because of their dramatic autumn migrations.

They breed in the conifer forests of Alaska and northern Canada, but when the nights start to lengthen and cool, these tiny birds begin an eight-thousand-kilometer migration from their breeding grounds all the way down to the Amazon River basin of South America.

The first stage of their journey takes them to the eastern shore of Canada and New England, U.S.A. Here the birds will congregate and ready themselves for the next stage, the most dangerous stage, of their annual migration south.

As the birds feed ravenously and add vital body fat in preparation for their journey, they instinctively wait for an approaching cold front with strong northwesterly winds on which they will ride far out to sea.

And when a cold front with these specific prevailing winds arrives, the blackpoll warblers take off. They leave in great flocks when it is night, flying out over the dark Atlantic Ocean heading directly for the distant continent of Africa.

This stage of their migration averages three thousand kilometers, and the small birds must fly non-stop for approximately eighty-eight hours over the Atlantic. There is no way for them to rest now; there is no way for them to feed. They must depend on their stored body fat and their inner strength to take them successfully to their journey's end.

But why do the birds fly en-masse in a southeasterly direction out to sea -- a direction that will not take them to South America?

Somewhere near the island of Bermuda, the birds pick up a prevailing trade wind. This trade wind will deflect the flocks of warblers, and they will now ride it to South America.

The birds fly inside this strong river of air until they reach sight of land once again, and now their colossal journey reaches its final stage as the birds continue on until they reach their winter feeding grounds within the great Amazon River basin.

Blackpoll warblers are famous for their stamina and for their strength, qualities that enable these tiny songbirds to traverse vast distances twice a year in their cycle of life.

Cloudsky hatched in the late spring many seasons ago. He was the lone baby to hatch out of three eggs that cold spring, and since he was the only baby, his mother and father lavished extra care on him and perhaps protected him too much.

When Cloudsky grew up and left the nest, it became obvious that he was somewhat fearful, a bit too fearful. However, his best friend, Treehopper, was exactly the opposite -- he was a bold and seemingly fearless little blackpoll warbler.

The first day Cloudsky met Treehopper, Treehopper lived up to his name!

They laughed and sang after meeting each other in a large spruce tree, and Treehopper asked Cloudsky if he had every hopped on every branch of a tree before. Of course, Cloudsky had never imagined such an endeavor; after all, any single tree has hundreds of branches.

But no adventure was too great for Treehopper.

Treehopper quickly hopped and flew from branch to branch, starting with the largest at the bottom of this particular spruce. Partly flying and partly hopping, as soon as he reached a branch he would flutter his wings and hop in a circle and sing out the count -- one, two, three…

Cloudsky was dumbfounded at first, but as Treehopper counted out the tenth branch he joined his friend in this new game. The warblers chased each other until they reached the top just as the sun was setting.

"One hundred and forty-four branches!" Treehopper and Cloudsky shouted together after they reached the topmost branch.

The two new friends watched the sun set over the distant, snow-covered mountains. As they watched, the sun etched long shadows over the distant peaks, and the endless line of white mountains transformed into pinkish-red, filled with dark shadows all along their mighty flanks.

A few days later, Treehopper surprised Cloudsky with a new challenge. "Let's fly to the top of the sky!"

"No one can do that," Cloudsky said simply. "The sky doesn't have a top."

"Let's go find out!" With a flash of his wings, Treehopper took off.

"Aren't you afraid of hawks or owls or something? I mean, there's no place to hide in the clear blue sky!" Cloudsky shouted after Treehopper, but either Treehopper didn't hear his frantic chattering, he didn't care, or he wasn't afraid. Treehopper continued flying higher and higher.

Now, Cloudsky was afraid. His parents had warned him to always be careful of predators, but he also was afraid to be alone. A few seconds later, his fear of being left all alone in the tree overwhelmed his fear of the unknown sky above.

"Wait for me!" Cloudsky shouted as he flew after Treehopper.

Treehopper circled above, waiting for Cloudsky. Together, they flew higher and higher, seeking the top of the sky.

The two warblers flew skyward as the winds carried them along, and soon both birds felt the air growing lighter, and they found it difficult to breathe.

Although Cloudsky was afraid, his beating heart also was filled with a burning fire that filled him with energy. They looked down and saw the canopy of trees blur into a single green maze below as even the rivers and fields grew smaller.

Eventually, however, they could fly no higher. Their wings could propel them no further, try as they might.

Treehopper cried out in frustration, singing of his great desire to touch the top of the sky. He cried out with sadness when he realized he had flown as high as he could.

"Don't cry, Treehopper. Look below us -- we have accomplished something almost as great."

Looking down, Cloudsky and Treehopper saw

islands of puffy clouds floating below.

"We've flown above the clouds! That's awesome!" Treehopper shouted with joy. Although they had failed to fly to the top of the sky, their flying above the clouds was enough to fill them with a sense of achievement.

All that summer, each day was a new adventure for Treehopper and Cloudsky. In the morning Cloudsky ate with his parents as fast as he could and then flew off to play with his best friend, and each evening, Cloudsky was the last bird to perch with his parents after he finally dragged himself away from Treehopper.

Then one day, the first cold winds from the artic blew across the forests of Alaska. It was time for the great migration south.

Cloudsky insisted that he and his parents fly in the same flock of warblers as Treehopper. He just couldn't bear to be parted from his best friend. Cloudsky and Treehopper's parents approved, and so they flew across the vast plains and forests of Canada heading for the eastern shoreline.

But now Cloudsky's fears returned.

As they flew farther and farther away from his nest tree, he wouldn't fly out of sight of the flock at any time. The land and trees around them were new and filled with unknown dangers. In fact, Cloudsky grew so fearful that some days he would not even seek out his friend but would stay near his parents, especially after they passed over the first towns and villages of man -- a new and fearful sight for the tiny bird.

At last, they arrived at the edge of the vast Atlantic Ocean.

Cloudsky and Treehopper stared out over the endless water that melted into the distant horizon far way, as if the ocean and sky became one somewhere at the edge of the world.

"I can't fly over that!" Cloudsky shouted with fear. "There is no end to the ocean! I'll grow tired and fall into the water and die!"

"All blackpoll warblers fly out over that water," Cloudsky's father said reassuringly. "You are young and strong. Just stay close to the flock, and all will be fine."

His parent's words calmed Cloudsky. In his heart, he vowed not to stray from the flock, for indeed, his greatest fear was to be alone. Now, however, that fear was replaced with a new one: the fear of finding himself both alone and lost over that great expanse of water -- and after flying in circles, lost and alone, falling into the cold waters and drowning.

As the days passed, Cloudsky began to feel better. There was plenty of food here in the land next to the ocean, and he again sought out his best friend.

On one particular day, Cloudsky went to play with Treehopper.

"Let's go play a trick on that mean cat in the yard over there, the one who scared us the other day," Treehopper suggested.

"Mom and Dad told me to stay far away from cats -- they can eat you!" Cloudsky protested.

"It'll be all right. Parents are too strict sometimes. We're too fast for an old tomcat."

"I don't know, Treehopper. My parents won't like it."

But no adventure and no challenge were too great for Treehopper.

The two warblers flew around to the backyard where the old yellow tabby roamed. Treehopper explained he was going to fly down and peck the old cat right between the ears and fly off.

Before Cloudsky could protest, Treehopper was off! With a flash of feathers, Treehopper soared right toward the cat and pecked him squarely between the ears.

"MEOW!" The cat shouted angrily.

This just made Treehopper laugh louder.

After a few moments, the cat continued walking, seemingly forgetting about the birds chirping excitedly in the trees above.

Treehopper made another daring dive, but just as Treehopper reached the cat, the cat whirled around and slapped the bird to the ground with his paw.

Cloudsky screamed shrilly in fright as he saw the cat step on his friend and then reach down, pick him up in his mouth, and shake him until feathers flew in the air. In his heart, Cloudsky realized his friend would die right before his eyes.

At first, Cloudsky froze with fear, not knowing what he could do. After all, what could a tiny warbler do against a cat? Suddenly, though, a memory flashed in his mind -- a cunning bird trick his parents had mentioned in a Song-Tale.

Cloudsky flew directly toward the cat and landed a few feet away.

"Oh, I'm hurt. My wing is broken!" Cloudsky began to hop frantically, flapping one wing while he held the other limp as if it were broken.

The cat stared at him with gleaming eyes with the still form of Treehopper hanging limply from his mouth.

"Oh, I cannot get away. I see a cat! What will I do?" Cloudsky chirped and whistled fearfully.

The cat lowered itself to leap, its tail whipping from side to side, but still it held Treehopper tight in its mouth.

Cloudsky hopped about faster and faster and cried even louder.

The prize before the cat became too much. Forgetting the bird in its mouth, the cat dropped the limp form down and crouched lower for the attack.

Cloudsky's heart beat faster than he thought it ever could.

The cat jumped.

Cloudsky flew off barely out of reach of its deadly claws, but he fluttered back to the ground a few feet away, hopping helplessly and quite tantalizingly near the cat.

Once again, the cat crouched and leaped for him.

Again Cloudsky waited until the last second and flew off a few feet and fluttered back to the ground. They repeated this dangerous game until both reached the edge of the fence. Cloudsky kept looking back, hoping his friend would fly up to a tree to safety, but the unmoving form of Treehopper lay silently where the cat had dropped him.

When the cat leaped again, Cloudsky flew high into the tree and circled back around, unseen by the cat. A few seconds later, Cloudsky landed next to Treehopper.

"Get up! We've got to fly away!" Cloudsky whistled urgently as he nudged at his friend.

Treehopper lay very still, only the gentle rising of his breast indicating he was still alive.

Suddenly, the cat saw both of them sitting on the ground. He crouched again, his eyes gleaming while his tail twitched with excitement.

"Get up! He's seen us!"

The cat attacked.

Cloudsky felt his fear overwhelm him now. He spread his wings in order to fly away, but he couldn't do it, not after he looked down at the helpless form of his best friend.

The cat bounded closer with each heartbeat. In a few seconds, both birds would be killed.

In that moment, Cloudsky grasped his friend with his feet and flapped his wings as hard as he could. They rose a few inches off the ground, and Cloudsky flapped his wings harder. The weight of his friend kept dragging him down, but Cloudsky would not let go.

"MEOW!"

Cloudsky didn't look back because he knew the cat was almost upon them. He beat his wings harder and harder, but although they flew forward, he couldn't get any lift to fly higher out of the cat's reach.

"MEOW!"

It sounded like the cat was right on top of them!

In his heart, Cloudsky knew the end had come for him and Treehopper -- this same day both would stop flying, and their parents would never know what had happened to them.

"MEOW!"

A stiff westerly breeze suddenly blew and lifted Cloudsky higher. Cloudsky felt the cat's claws brush the tips of his tail feathers, and then he was carrying Treehopper higher and higher until they flew into the protective trees beyond the yard.

Cloudsky tired quickly and landed on a wide branch.

"Wake up, Treehopper!" Cloudsky begged, but try as he might, he could not awaken his friend.

For the first time in his life, Cloudsky perched in a tree all night separated not only from his parents, but also from the flock, and yet, he would not leave his friend.

He fluffed out his feathers, trying to warm Treehopper from the cold winds that blew hard all through the night.

Unknown to Cloudsky, as the strong northwesterly winds blew harder and harder that night, the seething clouds of blackpoll warblers rose up into the night sky and flew out over the dark waters of the ocean.

Soon, all the warblers were far out at sea.

The next day, Treehopper woke hurt and

hungry. Cloudsky was so happy his friend was awake. But it quickly became evident that Treehopper was hurt and unable to fly. Treehopper groaned and closed his eyes to sleep again.

But Cloudsky discovered something worse than his friend's condition. When Cloudsky left him to go find his parents for help, he discovered all the flock gone. He returned with a heavy heart, now frightened by the prospect that he and his best friend were all alone.

When the sun reached its zenith in the sky, Treehopper awoke to find Cloudsky crying beside him.

"Ohhhhh, I hurt all over," Treehopper moaned as he tried to stretch.

"The flock has left us," Cloudsky whimpered fearfully.

"When did they leave?"

"Last night, while we perched in this tree."

"Then you must fly after them. You can still catch them if you fly fast and hard."

Cloudsky felt hope grow inside his heart.

"Go, Cloudsky. I'll catch up tomorrow. I know how you hate to be alone. I'll be fine. I'll… I'll catch up later..." Treehopper winced as he tried to spread his wings.

"I'll be looking for you!" Cloudsky hopped farther out on the branch. With a quick glance over his shoulder, he smiled at his friend and flew off toward the ocean.

He flew as fast as his little wings would beat. For the first time in his life, he flew through the sky alone.

He didn't like the feeling at all.

The wind still blew strongly, and soon Cloudsky reached the ocean, but as he looked around at the empty sea and sky, he felt his old fear fill his heart again.

He peered far out to sea, but as far as he could see there was nothing but water and sky.

There was no sign of any blackpoll warblers.

He knew Treehopper was right. If he flew fast enough on the current of the breeze he could probably catch the flock before sunset.

He knew he could do it, but his thoughts kept returning to his friend sitting hurt in a tree far behind.

Treehopper was now all alone in that tree.

As minute after minute passed, Cloudsky's heart became torn.

Deep inside, he felt the strong urging of instinct driving his wings with the added incentive of his fear.

But how would Treehopper feel tomorrow? It would take him two days to catch the flock if he felt well enough to fly. But what if he wasn't strong enough even then...

Cloudsky turned around.

He fought against the river of air, flying low to get under the strongest currents. Even more, he fought his fear and his powerful instinct, which tried to force him to continue the age-old migration of his kind.

But the love for his friend proved stronger.

As the sun sank low, Cloudsky landed on the branch next to Treehopper.

"Why did you come back?" Treehopper asked with surprise mixed with happiness.

"You are my best friend, Treehopper. I had to come back."

"But the flock is getting farther and farther away every minute."

"We'll fly together when you're better."

"Why?"

"We are best friends. I won't leave you, especially when you're hurt. Where you perch, I will perch, and where you fly, I will fly."

"What if we get lost? What if we die?" For the first time since Cloudsky had met him, Treehopper's courageous spirit failed him.

"We'll fly together. If we don't find the flock, we'll just have to make the journey on our own -- together." Cloudsky exuded quiet confidence, but inside, he still felt a twinge of fear at the thought of just Treehopper and him flying the vast ocean alone.

"You're a good bird, Cloudsky." Treehopper smiled weakly. "You'll have to lead the way."

Treehopper was hurt worse than they both feared. He couldn't fly, and so he couldn't get food for himself.

Cloudsky acted like a parent bird. Cloudsky found the berries and ate them, and then he came back to Treehopper and fed him as a parent feeds its babies. Treehopper's strength slowly returned. Each day he flexed his wings and grimaced with pain.

On the third day, Treehopper was able fly to another branch, and by the end of that same day, he could fly a short distance, but he didn't have the strength to start the long migration.

And now the strong wind no longer blew in the right direction.

"What are we going to do?" Treehopper asked sadly. "Every day, the flock gets farther away. They may have made it to the southern continent by now!"

"Another cold front will come. We will make the migration then." Cloudsky's confidence fed his friend's spirit.

Seven days after the flock left them, the wind again began to blow out of the northwest as another cold front approached. Treehopper felt much better and could fly with ease. The time seemed right. The two tiny birds readied themselves.

As the sun set behind them, the two young blackpoll warblers flew up into the night sky out over the mighty Atlantic. Neither bird had made this migration before, but they had the ingrained instinct of their ancestors written on their hearts, ancestors who had made this same migration for thousands of years.

They also felt the courage of their kind beating strong inside their feathered breasts.

But most of all, they had each other.

Cloudsky led Treehopper as they flew beyond the sight of land. They rode the strong winds and slowly gained altitude with each kilometer. Below them, they could hear the steady roar of the waves although they could not see the water through the darkness.

Cloudsky felt his fear rising again.

He felt so alone, and he was surrounded by strangeness.

"Cloudsky, how far do we fly in this direction before we turn?" Treehopper whistled from behind.

His friend's familiar voice calmed him.

He turned and smiled back at Treehopper. "*We will know.*"

The sun rose above the two tiny birds as they flew steadily toward the southeast. As they looked around, they realized the dark blue waters spread out in every direction with no end.

Neither bird spoke for a long time as they continued flying inside the river of air, but deep inside each bird, questions and fears wrestled violently with reason and instinct. Each was afraid to ask the other if they were flying in the right direction -- or had they already made a wrong turn?

They just kept flying.

As the sun set behind them that first day over the sea, they felt calm as their instinct took over. There was no turning back now. They had to find the place where the trade winds blew in the direction of their southern home, or else they would tire and fall from the sky.

Another night and day passed with the birds concentrating on flying at a steady pace, but with each hour, Cloudsky and Treehopper felt painful aching creep into their wings. As the exhaustion grew, so did their doubts and their fears.

175

When the sun rose for the third time, they saw a tiny rim of land far below -- they were passing over the island of Bermuda.

Something stirred inside their hearts, but their tiredness and fear muffled it .

"I think we should be close to the great river of air that will take us south," Cloudsky said with a hint of hope, peering down at the tiny spit of land.

"Are you sure?" Treehopper panted. "I'm s-s-so tired. Maybe we should fly down there and rest…"

"No!" Cloudsky shouted firmly. "We've got to fly higher!" he added with a conviction that surprised even him.

"I can't fly any higher. You'll have to go on without me, Cloudsky. Keep flying…"

Cloudsky slowed until he was flying wingtip to wingtip with Treehopper. He looked over at his friend. Treehopper's motions were jerky now, he 2was clearly struggling.

"Listen, I'll fly directly in front of you, just like the geese fly. Get in the air right behind me."

Treehopper closed his eyes and nodded.

Cloudsky sped up and got in formation right ahead of Treehopper. As he looked back over his shoulder, he saw his friend feel relief right away.

"Yes, that did help!" Treehopper smiled for the first time that day.

Cloudsky felt himself tiring, and worse, he felt his courage and confidence beginning to falter. Yet he knew that Treehopper depended on him now.

If he gave up, they would both die, and he

couldn't allow his friend to die.

"I'm flying higher -- stay in the window of air right behind me!" Cloudsky shouted.

The two small warblers rose higher and higher.

Night came again as the birds flew on and on. The darkness and their growing tiredness fueled their fear even more. Cloudsky was afraid to say anything now. Deep inside, he felt his hope beginning to fade away.

A terrible thought began growing inside Cloudsky's mind: somehow they had flown the wrong way. They were both lost, and it was his fault...

He felt the tears in his eyes, and he was glad the darkness hid them from Treehopper. He didn't want Treehopper to know that he had led them the wrong way.

He had failed...

All at once, they felt it at the same time.

Their feathers fluttered all over their bodies from a strong flow of air moving right above them. The river of air blew in the direction off to their right.

Their natural instinct sang out with joy, and somehow, almost magically, they both knew that they had reached the trade winds that would take them home!

"We've found it!" Cloudsky shouted triumphantly.

Treehopper could only manage a weak smile, and yet, as the birds turned into the comforting current of the mighty winds, both felt suddenly reenergized.

The river of air pushed and lifted the tiny birds. Within the grip of the invisible and mighty current, Cloudsky and Treehopper flew faster than they thought possible. The trade wind was aiding them, whisking them toward their ultimate destination.

"Higher, Treehopper. Higher! Let's go a little higher so the wind will push us even faster."

"I-I will try…"

Another day and night followed as the birds flew within the strong current of the trade winds. By the end of the second day on the new heading, their courage waned again as the aching tiredness returned. Both birds realized they were running out of energy, and if they didn't find land soon, they would fall into the sea.

But just as the sun reached its zenith the third day, they spotted a change on the distant horizon -- the coast of South America.

They flew faster now. Somehow the sight of their final destination pushed all fear and tiredness completely away, and then something wonderful happened -- they heard the songs of other blackpoll warblers.

It had not been until they had almost reached the trade winds over Bermuda that the parents of both Cloudsky and Treehopper realized their offspring were missing. Each set of parents had assumed the young birds were with the other parents in the initial confusion. It was too late to turn back for them, but the frantic parents convinced the flock to wait near the shore for the missing youngsters when they reached South America.

As day after day passed with no sign of them, their parents' hope fluttered and almost failed. While the sun was setting that very day, the leader of the flock had announced they would continue onward, since they figured that Cloudsky and Treehopper were not coming.

The joy of Cloudsky and Treehopper at finding the flock waiting for them in the leaves of the palm trees was indescribable.

The most happy and joyous song that any bird had heard in many a year rang out through the trees and up into the air.

Every bird who heard the song about little Cloudsky and his best friend, Treehopper, repeated it immediately in its own dialect. It was a simple song about the bond of friendship that enabled two tiny birds to complete one of the longest and most dangerous migrations known.

The song traveled with the wind, chasing the setting sun.

The next morning, as the sun rose over the ocean beyond the palm trees where Cloudsky and Treehopper perched with their parents, they heard a seagull sing from far out on the sea.

The seagull sang of them -- the friendship and courage of Cloudsky and Treehopper.

A new Song-Tale had traveled around the entire world in a single day and entered the realm of legend among all the birds.

Chapter Fourteen

Bluesky dreamed about Cloudsky and Treehopper that night.

He dreamed both were his friends while they played in the trees and flew up above the clouds. He also dreamed they made the great migration south together.

When he awoke, he felt an aura of happiness that slowly faded along with the memory of his beautiful dream.

"How are Mama's babies this morning? Time to wake up! A new day is here!" Sunshine chirped merrily.

"Let's go find Funwind and play." Cloudshadow stretched his wings and yawned.

Bluesky's sorrow returned.

"I think I'll just stay here today." He hung his head in a forlorn manner.

"Why don't you want to play with your new friends, Bluesky?" Sunshine hopped onto the branch next to Bluesky and Cloudshadow.

Bluesky looked down and sighed, but he couldn't lie to his mother. So, he explained how Funwind had taken him aside and told him that he and his friends liked Cloudshadow and Songjoy but they thought he was weird and didn't want to play with him.

He looked away from his mother as he told her the rest of the story, how Funwind drove him away and played with the other birds.

"That's terrible!" Sunshine said with more than a hint of anger in her voice. "I mean, just because you only have one leg, that's no reason not to play with you. He played with your brother and sister."

"What's the matter?" Treetop flew up and settled on a nearby branch.

Sunshine quickly reviewed the happenings of yesterday, emphasizing the injustice done to Bluesky.

"Young birds can be cruel." Treetop sighed. "His dad was the same way when we were young, taunting others and hurting their feelings made him feel superior somehow. He still has a sharp tongue even to this day. It's his way of dominating other birds."

"Youngsters don't realize that words can hurt as much as real wounds. Sometimes they can hurt more." Sunshine frowned.

"They can hurt more than the sharpest talons. My most painful memories when I was young are of other birds ridiculing me." Treetop took a deep breath and shrugged.

"I'm sorry, I never knew that," Sunshine said. She paused a moment and continued. "Well, what are we going to do about this?"

"I guess we need to do something," Treetop said with an unsure tone. He sighed deeply.

"Of course we need to do something! Not only did they call Bluesky 'weird', but they made him leave while they all went off to play more!" Sunshine hopped angrily on the branch, her long tail flipping up and down in agitation.

181

"I guess none of them should go play with them." Treetop cocked his head and watched for Sunshine's reaction.

"No, I think all of them should go play with them, and Cloudshadow and Songjoy will make sure the others play with Bluesky too."

"I don't know ... you can't make other birds play with you, if they don't want to."

"Then they'll come back here with us."

Bluesky watched in dismay as his parents argued back and forth. He felt even more embarrassed and sad. After all, this was his fault. If he didn't look so different from other birds, they wouldn't make fun of him.

His parents finally agreed that all three of them would eat breakfast first. After that, the three of them could go play with Funwind and his friends if they wanted. However, if Funwind called Bluesky names or tried to make him leave, Cloudshadow and Songjoy were to leave too.

Bluesky didn't feel any better about it, but he decided he would try. He kept thinking about the story last night and wanted to make friends, but he was afraid of another cruel rejection.

While they hunted bugs in the grass near each other, Bluesky looked over at his mother. "Do you think I will have a friend like Treehopper one day?"

"Sure you will, Bluesky. Just be yourself -- others will like you."

"Funwind doesn't like me."

"Give him time."

Bluesky found a few bugs and ate them in

silence. His mother's words gave him hope -- a faint hope.

Songjoy, Cloudshadow, and Bluesky flew toward the trees where they had met Funwind and the others yesterday. As soon as the three alighted on a branch, Funwind and Eveningbreeze flew up.

"Have you come to play with us again?" Funwind asked with a twinkle in his eyes, but when he noticed Bluesky with them, his expression changed.

"Why did you bring him?" Eveningbreeze asked with contempt.

"He's our brother," Cloudshadow said defensively. "We play together."

"He's so weird-looking. It creeps me out looking at him." Eveningbreeze stared at Bluesky's missing leg.

Bluesky lowered his head in shame.

"He's not weird-looking," Cloudshadow said with an angry edge to his voice. "He's got two wings; he can fly as well as any of us."

"But he can't walk like us," Eveningbreeze said simply. "And he's always fluttering his wings like he's afraid. He's so... pitiful."

"What if we don't want to play with him?" Funwind challenged.

"Then we don't play either." Songjoy hopped over and stood beak to beak with Funwind, daring him to say anything else about her baby brother.

Funwind and Eveningbreeze exchanged glances.

"Okay, we'll let the poor, one-legged bird play with us -- *if he can*."

Songjoy and Cloudshadow looked at each other a moment and then at Bluesky, who shrugged and then nodded his acceptance of their deal. Cloudshadow also nodded his agreement.

"Okay, we'll play with you as long as Bluesky is included."

"Sure, let's *all* play," Funwind said with a high pitched voice.

Bluesky heard the condescending tone more than he heard Funwind's words. In spite of the invitation to play, he was suspicious. He steeled himself for trouble – and for more pain.

"Follow us if you can," Eveningbreeze called out as he and Funwind took flight.

Songjoy, Cloudshadow, and Bluesky gave chase.

The five young mockingbirds flew in and out of the canopy of trees. It was a typical game of "fly and chase" with Eveningbreeze the first bird being chased. Everyone was soon singing and chirping happily. Everyone took turns being 'it' except Bluesky, but he didn't mind; he simply enjoyed playing and being with his new friends.

After a while, they all sat on the same branch, out of breath and resting from their exertions. Funwind sat next to Bluesky. As everyone caught their breath, Funwind leaned closer to Bluesky.

"You want us to chase you next?" Funwind asked.

"I-I guess so," Bluesky said hesitantly.

"You're not afraid are you?"

"No!" Bluesky said firmly.

184

Funwind nodded and smiled. He yawned and slowly stretched his wings; then, suddenly, he jerked as if he had lost his balance and bumped hard into Bluesky.

"Ahhhh!" Bluesky cried out. He fluttered his wings frantically, trying to regain his balance but fell over onto his side and almost over the edge of the branch.

Funwind and Eveningbreeze howled with laughter as they pointed at Bluesky, who hurriedly tried to stand back up, but in his embarrassment, he rushed his movements and fell again.

"You're such a dork!" Eveningbreeze laughed harshly.

"Doesn't he look stupid!" Funwind added. "He's always fluttering his wings like he's scared."

"You did that on purpose!" Songjoy shouted angrily.

"See how easy he fell over. A bird needs two legs." Funwind laughed even harder.

"He's a freak," Eveningbreeze added sharply.

"Yeah, he's a one-legged freak!" Funwind laughed.

Bluesky finally got himself back up. He fluffed out his feathers in an effort to feel better, but his embarrassment only grew more uncomfortable as their harsh laughter continued.

He looked away with tears in his eyes.

"Let's see how you like it!" In a flash of movement, Songjoy flew across the branch and bumped into Funwind so hard she knocked a couple of his feathers off.

"Owwww!" Funwind toppled over on his side but immediately hopped upright. He scowled at Songjoy, who scowled right back at him.

"Doesn't feel so good when it happens to you, eh?" Songjoy said sarcastically.

"Do that again, and I'll knock you out of this tree," Funwind growled.

"I'd like to see you try!"

Funwind turned and stared at Bluesky, who still could not bring himself to look him in the eyes.

"Every bird knows that the dumbest and plainest birds are the sparrows -- little brown runts who chatter away as if they don't have any sense," Funwind said with an arrogant tone. "Stupid little brown birds, that's what sparrows are."

"And they all look alike!" Eveningbreeze chattered.

"And next are those plain, ugly Mourning Doves. Always singing those sad songs -- yuck," Funwind said. "Dumb birds."

Eveningbreeze and Funwind looked at each other with a conspiratorial gleam.

"But a one-legged bird is the dumbest-looking bird in the entire world," Funwind said harshly.

Bluesky started crying. He couldn't help it; the tears poured out of his eyes. He just felt so terribly sad.

Songjoy and Cloudshadow looked at Bluesky with open beaks. Bluesky took wing and flew as fast as he could back to his parents.

Songjoy glared angrily at the two birds who were still laughing. "The dumbest birds in the world are you two. Don't bother asking me to play with you anymore -- I'll never play with either of you again!" Songjoy turned to fly.

"We don't want to be near your deformed brother anyway. So, fly away, little dumb birds -- far away!" Funwind laughed even harder as Songjoy's eyes narrowed in anger.

Songjoy and Cloudshadow flew after their brother.

Treetop and Sunshine were first saddened and then grew angry when Songjoy related what happened. The parents decided it best for them not to play with Funwind anymore after they heard the ugly names he called Bluesky.

"Who will we play with?" Cloudshadow asked.

Treetop and Sunshine looked at each other in surprise.

"Well, maybe it's time to start perching in another tree. You'll meet other mockingbirds then, and some of them can be your friends," Treetop said.

"What if they think I look stupid? What if they make fun of me?" Bluesky asked with a hint of sadness.

"There, there. They won't say things like that. Not all birds will be like that terrible little Funwind," Sunshine chirped comfortingly.

Bluesky noticed his mother look toward his father for support, but Treetop quickly looked away.

After their afternoon feeding, the family of five took flight and soared several houses down the street toward the old oak tree. This particular oak was the oldest tree left after the subdivision was built fifteen years ago. It was also the most popular tree this side of Lake Monroe.

Treetop led his family into the middle branches of the great oak. The gnarled branches grew all around the thick trunk and formed a circular canopy of green leaves. The oak stood apart from the nearest trees in an empty lot on the farthest street of the subdivision. Before the ancient tree, the houses and streets stretched out in three directions.

Behind its green canopy, the last vestiges of the once vast forest still stood proudly. Back then, the great forest flourished on either side of the waters of Anneewakee Creek and the trees grew uninterrupted southward until it joined the Chattahoochee River. The forest continued on either side of the Chattahoochee as it flowed on its journey to distant Lake Seminole. The forest ended at the lake, but the river continued southward until it joined the Flint River and became the Apalachicola River and finally spilled into Apalachicola Bay in the Gulf of Mexico

The mighty oak stood like a silent sentinel apart from the other trees as if guarding the last trees of the forest from the onslaught of houses, and upon its many branches birds of all families found food and protection and abundant places to roost for the night.

Treetop and Sunshine landed near a thick growth of leaves on one branch. Songjoy, Cloudshadow, and Bluesky landed moments later and quickly hopped closer.

Bluesky loved the tree as soon as he saw it. As he looked around at the network of branches, he heard the happy songs of many different kinds of birds.

Everyone that lived here was happy.

As he and his family hopped around and ate a few bugs and began to settle in, Bluesky noticed a change in the birds around them. At first, the birds flew and hopped around going about their own business, but now he noticed how some stopped and stared at him and his family. He could see them whispering together as they nodded in his direction. If he caught them looking, they quickly turned away in embarrassment.

Bluesky felt his familiar sadness return.

Still, he put on a brave front. He saw his mother and father smiling and cheerful once again. The change seemed to be helping them. They were no longer arguing and bickering like they had been recently, and both Songjoy and Cloudshadow were playing with a couple of new mockingbirds a few branches away.

Bluesky started to join them and meet these new friends, but he decided to stay. He figured it might be best if he let them make friends first. Perhaps later he would meet them and they might want to play with him too. He hoped.

As the sun sank toward the western horizon, all the birds began to settle down and seek out a good perch for the night.

Bluesky perched near his family next to the great trunk as the light faded. Other birds sat on the same branch farther out near the leaves. Just as they all started to get sleepy, two mockingbirds hopped down near them.

One of the birds was Aunt Coldrain.

"Excuse us, dearies."

"W-hat? Oh, Aunty Coldrain," Treetop said with uneasy recognition. "It's, uh… good to see you here."

"Yes, and I have Bigclouds with me."

"Nice to meet you," Treetop said cordially.

"Yes, indeed." However, Bigclouds did not sound as if he were pleased to meet them.

"What can we do for you?" Sunshine smiled sweetly. "Do you want to perch near us? If so, you are more than welcome."

"Actually," Coldrain began. "We've been sent as envoys."

"That sounds so -- official." Sunshine said with rising suspicion.

"It is. You see, the other birds that live in this tree are… uh, *concerned* by your presence."

"What do you mean?" Treetop was now wide awake. He hopped closer to the two envoys.

"I'll get right to the point. We'd rather your family find another tree in which to perch," Bigclouds said gruffly.

"We have every right to perch in this tree just as any other bird!" Anger laced Treetop's words. "Birds don't own trees. If there is room, any bird can perch in any tree. That is the way of birds since the beginning!"

"Yes, that's true -- in *most* cases." Coldrain's

voice now took on a condescending tone. "The other birds have noticed your poor, pitiful, one-legged baby…"

"Bluesky!" Sunshine shouted in her frustration. "He does have a name, you know."

"Yes, yes, I know. I mean, who would have thought a one-legged bird would have lived this long, much less able to fly. It's so odd to watch him hopping around awkwardly, much less…"

"He can hear just fine, you know! And he can see and he can fly!" Sunshine said angrily, still trying to keep a semblance of control. "Please, don't talk about him as if he's not present. Other than having one leg, he's normal, and he's a *good bird*."

"Why, I'm sure he… well, I guess… oooooh, that's not why we're here."

"Are you asking us to leave?"

Treetop hopped right in front of Coldrain who hopped back one step in surprise.

"Not tonight -- it's already dark -- but tomorrow we would like you to go find another tree, and while you're here, please… well, you know, don't get too close to any of us. Especially…" Coldrain nodded over at Bluesky with a look of distaste.

"What's the matter? Are they afraid one of *your* legs might fall off if he gets too close?" Treetop asked with bitter sarcasm.

"Well!" Coldrain cocked her head as if she had been insulted. "It's not exactly that…"

Sunshine's countenance clouded even more, but just as she was about to reply, another mockingbird

191

flew up.

"Windday!" Treetop's voice echoed both joy and fondness.

Sunshine smiled proudly.

"Hi, Mom. Hi, Dad." Windday looked at the three smaller mockers sitting on the branch next to them. As his glance fell upon Bluesky, his gaze traveled briefly down to his missing leg. He looked deeply into Bluesky's eyes with a strange familiarity.

"Who is this?" Cloudshadow asked with puzzlement.

"This is your big brother," Sunshine said proudly. "He was born last season, first-born of our second brood."

"Big brother!" Songjoy warbled happily.

Windday looked over at Coldrain and Bigclouds.

"Will you abide by what the other birds ask?" Bigclouds waited, tapping his foot impatiently.

"I guess so," Treetop replied. "I don't really know what to say. I've never known birds to ostracize other birds like this. It's... unheard of."

"*It's discrimination*!" Sunshine added.

"You've got to remember, strange things have been happening the last few seasons. Eggs don't hatch. Babies are born deformed and soon die." Bigclouds stared at Bluesky.

"Why, we've heard that in one grove of trees near the lake that not a single egg hatched this season! It scared the parents so badly that they didn't try to lay any more eggs this season."

Coldrain shook her head in an exaggerated fashion to indicate her shock and revulsion while she continued to glance nervously at Bluesky's missing leg.

"Okay, we'll keep our distance -- for now." Treetop hopped closer to his family. "We would like to visit with Windday. So, if you could both leave…"

"Well! I never." Coldrain turned and flew away in a huff. Bigclouds took one last look at Bluesky, and then he too flew back to his perch.

"Oh, that Coldrain! She makes me so mad." Sunshine groaned.

"Nobody likes Coldrain." Treetop sighed with frustration.

"She's so critical. She finds fault with everything."

"Her parents were like that," Treetop said with a sigh. "Everything was black and white with them. They were very stern birds, especially in the way they raised Coldrain. They wanted only the best for her, but they wound up building a barrier between themselves and almost everyone else."

"No one was good enough for them." Sunshine said, following his train of thought.

"Exactly. Now Coldrain is cynical like them. In fact, she's more so since she never found a mate that lived up to her standards. Every prospective mate she ever met fell short. She always found something wrong them."

She made her nest, now she'll have to sit in it - all by herself." Sunshine grimaced.

"Yes, it's her own fault. She can't even see that she's the reason for her own loneliness, it makes her even more severe in her dealings with others." Treetop shrugged.

"If she comes around me again with bad words for us or our fledglings, I'm going to give her a swift kick on the rump!" Sunshine's eyes narrowed.

"Now Sunshine, remember, *she's family*."

"Then I'll give her two swift kicks and a peck on the head."

Treetop and Sunshine looked at each other a moment in silence. And then both chuckled under their breath, as if they were sharing some mischievous secret.

"You know, she really does think she's doing what's best," Treetop added.

"But she's wrong!" Sunshine said with conviction. "There's nothing wrong with Bluesky. There's nothing wrong with our family. And there's certainly no reason for them to be afraid of him or us!"

"I know. But, they view him… they view us *differently* from others. They think we're, um, well… "

Sunshine waited for Treetop to complete the sentence. She couldn't even guess what he was about to say this time. The seconds passed slowly, but he simply stood there. She felt her emotions begin to boil.

"It doesn't matter what they think of us." She said with a hint of anger.

Treetop slowly shook his head and then turned

away. He sighed deeply and stood with his back to her. Finally, he turned around to face her.

"I know, it shouldn't matter. But, it bothers me what others think of us. *It really bothers me.*" He whispered the last sentence with emphasis, his expression one of great somberness.

Sunshine's heart pounded with surprise and confusion. She stared speechless at Treetop a moment.

"Don't let them worry you, Mom. You too, Dad." Windday smiled at Treetop and Sunshine.

"It's so good to see you." Sunshine had completely forgotten about Windday. Her expression softened. "Do you live over here now?"

"Yes." Windday smiled. "I like to perch in this old tree a lot, but I don't do it every night."

"Why are the birds here treating us like... like we have some kind of disease?" Treetop's anger overflowed.

"When they saw a bird with only one leg, it made them afraid."

"Afraid of what?"

"Just like they said, strange things are happening more and more. There's fear in the air -- fear of the unknown, of some kind of impending doom, and seeing a one-legged bird puts it out in the open. It puts a face to the fear, so to speak."

Treetop and Sunshine exchanged alarmed glances.

"I don't like it when they stare at my missing leg, Mama. It makes me feel..." Bluesky let out a sigh of sadness.

195

"Don't cry, baby," Sunshine said. "We love you."

Bluesky smiled in sad kind of way.

That evening as the stars twinkled in the clear heavens over the oak, Windday caught up with his parents and got to know his younger siblings. It was a happy visit for all of them.

Bluesky realized for the first time that while young birds in their hatching year stayed close to their parents as they taught them the essentials of life, once a new season came, young birds left their parents and flew out on their own. That was the reason he had not seen any of his siblings from his parent's first brood that season. Once they had learned how to hunt and feed themselves, young birds flew off to find their own way.

This thought frightened Bluesky.

He listened while Windday told them what he had done the past year. Windday had made friends with a lot of mockingbirds, although he had not taken a mate this season. He seemed quite happy and content and even related a few adventures he experienced with his new friends.

Once again, Bluesky yearned to make friends -- and to have a friend like Treehopper -- but no Mockingbird liked him, no one except his family.

And yet, that was all he really needed, he realized.

He decided that even when he grew into an adult mockingbird, he would stay close to both his parents and Cloudshadow and Songjoy. They were all he needed, and maybe Windday and he could become friends too.

Windday decided to perch with them that night, and it brought a sense of joy to all.

As the six mockingbirds slowly settled down, Bluesky studied his family one by one. Each bird in his family perched with eyes shut, their expressions one of rest and peacefulness.

When he looked at his father, though, he noticed the strained look on his face. Bluesky knew his father was bothered by the brutal attitude of the others more so than anyone, and he hated it that his parents argued more and more, though they tried to keep it from them.

Bluesky felt even worse because he knew they argued about him. Not about him directly, but because the other birds avoided them all because of him. He knew his parents were deeply bothered by the condescending stares and constant murmuring all directed at Bluesky. All of their problems were due to him and his birth defect, and it made Bluesky feel terrible inside. He loved his family more than anything.

A sudden realization gripped his heart and caused him to groan out loud: he realized that all the other birds hated his family *because of him*.

Perhaps he should leave his parents when he was grown; then he wouldn't be a burden to them and they wouldn't argue any more. In fact, the other birds would no longer have a reason to hate them when he was gone. Yes, he would fly out on his own when it was time.

Maybe …

Chapter Fifteen

Mark sat at the breakfast table with a steaming cup of coffee and a small pair of binoculars.

The early morning sun streamed across the backyard in filtered rays as it passed through the stand of trees beyond his backyard fence. The small grove of trees provided a natural barrier on two sides of his property from the other houses in the subdivision while a wooden privacy fence lined the remaining side.

It was Saturday morning, but Mark still liked to get up at his normal time of six o'clock and drink a cup of coffee alone before the kids or Jane woke up. Drinking coffee each morning was one of life's little pleasures he particularly enjoyed. He loved to first breathe in the rich aroma -- savor it a delicious moment -- before taking a sip and feeling the warm glow spread inside his body. He would hold the steaming cup of liquid near his face, letting the heady perfume build anticipation before each sip.

After the kids and his wife woke up and came downstairs, he would visit with them a few minutes and enjoy their company and conversation. He loved to spend ten minutes or so just talking with his family as everyone got ready for the day. Jane would sip her coffee and mention her plans for the day or maybe talk about a book she was reading while the kids giggled over their cereal.

Even on weekdays he tried not to rush his mornings with his family, but Saturday and Sunday mornings were better since he could enjoy everything at his leisure and especially since he could spend some 'quiet time' before the others awakened and the day really began.

He sipped his coffee, closing his eyes to allow his other senses maximum enjoyment.

He simply relaxed and watched the birds come up to his feeders next to the bay window. From time to time, he would use his binoculars and see what kind of birds were feeding on the ground farther out in the yard.

His mother had taught him the joy of birdwatching. She had also passed along the joy of flowers and plants, but perhaps her greatest gift to him was the joy of reading. Mark didn't have as much time to read as he once did. Still, he found time to read several novels each year -- mostly science fiction, his favorite genre, or sometimes a good mystery or an adventure novel.

He also made it a practice to read one biography each year. He found a special satisfaction in reading about the lives and accomplishments of some outstanding individual, a pleasure he learned from school assignments long ago. Last year, he'd enjoyed reading a biography about Paul McCartney and the previous year one of Mozart. On his bed stand awaited a book about William Shakespeare, his biography project for this year. He'd already read several biographies based on Shakespeare's life, but he never seemed to get enough of 'The Bard.'

He also loved to read the Bible. He tried to read

one chapter every day, and at the very least, he read one verse each day.

As he sat quietly at kitchen table, he heard the faint laughter of Philip and Katie running down the stairs.

He loved to hear children laugh, and he couldn't help chuckling to himself as his kids came bounding down the stairs with their childish laughter filling the air.

"What's going on?" Mark said with a smile after they burst into the kitchen.

"Katie's tickling me!" Philip squealed with renewed laughter as Katie put her arms around him and tickled him again.

"Pretty soon, you'll be big enough to tickle her back." Mark laughed.

"He can do it already!" Katie said. "Except I can still run faster and get away from him when I want to."

"I can catch you!" Philip said with a suddenly serious tone.

"Okay!" Mark said, still chuckling. "Do you two want some cereal?"

"What are you doing, Dad?" Philip noticed the small binoculars on the table next to his cup of coffee.

"Drinking coffee and watching birds."

The little boy went over to his father and crawled up in his lap. He leaned over the table, picked up the binoculars, and held them up to his eyes.

Mark laughed again as he reached down, turned

them around the correct way, and gently put them up to Philip's eyes. He showed him how to turn the focus adjustment and pointed him toward the bird feeder out in the yard.

"It's all fuzzy!" Philip moaned.

"Here, let me adjust it slowly while you look." Mark carefully turned the focus adjustment and asked Philip each time if it was better. Finally, the little boy uttered a satisfied 'wow.'

"I see a bird real close. This thing is great, Dad."

Katie came over and leaned against her father while Philip continued to watch the birds through the binoculars.

Mark allowed Katie a turn to see the birds feasting on the seeds, and as they watched, Buddy the cat sauntered into the kitchen.

"Buddy!" Philip squealed as he jumped down and picked up the cat.

Mark and Jane had gotten Buddy last year when he was a kitten. He had grown into a fine looking young cat and seemed to enjoy the children's attention as well as allowing them to pick him up without complaint.

That had been the main reason for getting another cat. KC was older and didn't like being picked up anymore, which the kids longed to do each time they saw her. She would *meow* her complaints against the action and had even hissed a few times if the children ignored her warning. Now the kids knew that KC only wanted to be petted and that Buddy liked both petting and being held.

Whereas KC had short fur that was jet-black and pure white, Buddy was one quarter Himalayan and had long, silky fur the color of charcoal.

"Meoooowww," Buddy cried. His meow was different than KC's meow. It almost sounded like Buddy was saying "noooooo" at times.

Philip hugged Buddy tighter and then put him down so he could eat out of his bowl.

KC pattered into the kitchen at the sound of Buddy's crunching his food.

"I remember when we got Buddy last year," Katie said while she put down the binoculars. "When did you and Mom get KC?"

"One day your mom had gone for a walk by herself while I changed the oil in the car." Mark smiled with the fond memory. "When she came back, this tiny kitten was following her, doing its best to keep up with her. Your mother told me she had saved the kitten from a patch of kudzu!"

Mark watched as his children's eyes opened wide with surprise.

"Mom saved KC's life? How?" Philip asked in awe.

"The little kitten had wandered away from its mother and had gotten lost in a big patch of kudzu and couldn't find her way out. As your mother passed by on the road, she heard the little kitten crying plaintively for help. So, your mother stopped and called to her. The kitten came to her voice and escaped!" Mark smiled at his slight embellishments to the fond story.

"And so, KC followed her home because Mom

saved her life. Wow, Mom is a hero!" Philip exclaimed.

"Yes. When I got done changing the oil, I picked her up and carried her to every house near the kudzu patch trying to find her home, but no one claimed her. Well, she was so cute, and when no one claimed her, I brought her back and we kept her."

"I like that story." Philip laughed.

"It's true too, and in a way, KC chose us as her family."

"What does KC stand for?" Philip said, hugging Mark's arm tight.

"Kansas City, of course!" Katie laughed knowingly.

"Well, not exactly." Mark laughed heartily at his daughter's words.

"What does KC really stand for then?" Katie asked with a puzzled expression.

"Well, your mom and I didn't really pin it down to one thing." Mark smiled. "It could stand for 'Kudzu Cat.' Or, it could mean 'Krazy Cat' since she was so funny back then. Or..."

"Or what?" Philip and Katie said together.

"KC could mean 'Kitty Cat.' Your mom and I thought of many names for several days, and we finally agreed on KC, not really knowing what KC meant, although it could mean any of those!"

"I like KC. I wish she would let me pick her up." Katie reached down and rubbed KC's ears, causing her to purr contentedly. Then she looked up and asked, "Are the birds our pets too?"

"In a way, except they are still wild and free. KC and Buddy live with us, and we feed and care for them, but we only feed the birds -- they come and go as they please. Because we feed them, they stay close to our house and even build nests near us, so we get the pleasure of seeing them regularly."

"It looks like the same birds come every day to eat your seeds, Dad." Philip pointed as a bird flew up to the feeder just outside the window. The tiny chickadee reached inside and grabbed a black sunflower seed; with a quick glance at them, he flew off to a nearby branch to eat it.

"Mainly five kinds of birds come to this feeder outside the window. You remember seeing the bright yellow bird with black wings?"

"Yes! I like them. They're pretty birds." Katie cried gleefully.

"That's a goldfinch."

Suddenly, as if on cue, two goldfinches alighted on the feeder.

"Look closer ... see the white wing-bar in the middle of his black wing?"

"I see it, Daddy!" Katie shouted with glee.

"Notice the alternating white feathers at his wing tips too, and on his tail."

"They're so yellow, it looks like they glow!" Philip laughed.

"See his head." Mark pointed. "He wears a black cap on his forehead. Goldfinches are pretty birds."

In a flurry of wings, two more birds alighted on the feeder along with the goldfinches.

"Those are the goldfinches' cousin, the house finch, a male and a female. They resemble a big sparrow with brown and tan feathers streaked all over their body, especially the female. The male has raspberry-red feathers on his head and neck and chest, and his beak is short and thick because he mostly eats seeds."

"What are those two?" Katie pointed as a tiny bird perched on the top of the feeder along with a second, slightly larger bird. Both birds glanced down at the other birds eating seed as if waiting their turn.

"That's a Carolina Chickadee. He's one of the smallest birds."

The two children peered through the window.

"I like his face the best." Katie proclaimed.

"Yes, he's quite handsome. See the black feathers on top of his head and his neck -- his black cap and black bib -- and notice the pure white feathers on his cheeks that narrow to a point right at his tiny black beak."

"It looks like a racing stripe!" Philip laughed.

"Yes, I never thought of it quite like that." Mark chuckled in delight.

"What about the gray bird?" Katie pointed at the other bird, who appeared to be searching for just the right seed.

"That's the chickadee's cousin, the Tufted Titmouse. He's covered with mouse-gray feathers with a small patch of red on his sides and a whitish belly, and on top of his head is a little crest." Mark pointed as the titmouse raised his feathered crest as if to show it off for his newfound audience.

"Only a few birds have a crest of feathers like the Tufted Titmouse," Mark explained. "The blue jay has one, as does one of my favorite birds."

"Which one?" Katie and Philip asked together.

"It's also your grandmother's favorite bird -- the Northern Cardinal."

"That's the *really* red bird, right, Daddy?" Katie asked as she put a pudgy little finger to her chin.

"Yes, that's the one."

"What are ya'll doing?" Jane yawned as she walked into the kitchen. She reached down and kissed Mark on his lips in greeting and squatted down and hugged each child. "How about an omelet for breakfast this morning?" she asked.

On weekends Jane liked to fix them all a hot breakfast, which they ate together at the kitchen table while the cats ate out of their bowls and the birds came and went at the feeder.

"Sure, honey, and maybe some bacon?"

Mark went up and took his shower while the children put on their clothes and started watching cartoons as Jane cooked.

Jane was sipping coffee at the kitchen table when Mark came back down fresh and clean from his shower.

"Did you read that article in the newspaper?" Jane asked with a note of urgency.

"The one about the miscarriages?"

"Yes, it sounds like the EPA and DNR are kind of blowing this off as a non-issue."

"Well, they discussed the annual tests they perform on the air, water table, and the ground soil at every landfill in the state, and nothing out of the ordinary has ever been noted on any of them. They did some extra testing around our county the last two weeks because of the growing concern. They reported that all came up normal." Mark poured himself a third cup of coffee.

"But something's wrong. Women are having miscarriages -- too many!"

"I have some news of my own, honey. John Sanders has a friend in the DNR. He has family who lives in our county, so he's concerned with this as much as we are." Mark put his arm around Jane's shoulder and squeezed comfortingly. "This friend of John's said he would dig into the records and give us a report on every business that ever dumped chemicals or stored them around here in the past."

"You think it's some kind of toxic chemical causing this?" Jane's voice was edged with fear.

"I don't know, but there's no major factory near us, no smokestacks, and no waste products from a source like that. The newspaper said all local farms and produce are being tested and coming up clean. Everything that's being tested is fine, but something is causing this. Well, after talking to some of the guys at work, we wondered if a company may have dumped something in the past and forgot about it, and maybe it's leaking now."

"I thought the EPA and DNR said they tested all the sites annually?"

Mark took a sip. He looked up at his wife and grimaced.

"Might be something not registered as a landfill or a dump site. Unless it was identified or registered as hazardous material when it was dumped or stored, then it wouldn't be tested... and then it could get into the air or the water if it began leaking..."

Mark saw his wife's eyes widen with fear.

"Something like Love Canal back in the seventies? I remember they built an entire subdivision over an old landfill that had toxic waste, and then years later people started getting cancer and... and dying..." Jane whispered fearfully.

"Something like that."

"Oh, Mark!"

***

Our Feathered Friends of the Southeast
A. C. Wages

Northern Cardinal
Latin: *Cardinalis cardinalis*

(excerpt)

A medium-sized songbird covered with brilliant scarlet feathers all over its body and sporting a jaunty crest of the same color with a black face and black eyes. His heavy orange beak contrasts with the gorgeous red

208

feathers of his body and the black feathers of his face. The female is identical except she is covered with tan feathers, although she is graced with a smidgen of red feathers on her wings and tail.

The cardinal is commonly called redbird, Virginia nightingale, and cardinal-bird.

This popular songster is common throughout the Southeast and a frequent visitor at bird feeders. The cardinal's call is a spritely *chip chip chip*. When the redbird sings from on high, its song is a series of clear and slightly slurred whistles followed at the end by a delightfully melodic trill.

If you keep your feeders well stocked with seed, it is easy to attract a number of cardinals. These birds are territorial and will remain near your yard when they realize food is available. Their bright plumage makes them easy to spot and enjoy.

This author has many times paused while standing out in the yard and enjoyed one of these beautiful birds as he sang enthusiastically from a nearby branch. Especially in the early mornings during the spring and summer, the air is filled with the crystal-clear notes of these wonderful singers.

The Cherokee word for 'redbird' is *dotsuwa* (doh-joo-wah). Three types of redbirds live in the Southeast, the homeland of the Cherokee. These three redbirds are the Scarlet Tanager, the Summer Tanager, and the Northern Cardinal, but the term *dotsuwa* is used exclusively by the Cherokee in reference to the cardinal alone. He is the most common redbird and the greatest singer of the three. The cardinal plays an important role in many ancient Cherokee tales, especially in their myths of Creation.

The cardinal is the official state bird of seven states: Illinois, Indiana, Kentucky, North Carolina, Ohio, Virginia, and West Virginia. More states have chosen the Northern Cardinal as a state bird than any other bird. In addition, a major league baseball team, the St. Louis Cardinals; an NFL team, the Arizona Cardinals; and a number of college teams are named after this beautiful and energetic bird.

Chapter Sixteen

The next few weeks were difficult.

Everywhere Treetop and Sunshine led their children, they were met with suspicion and fear. Treetop tried to find a place where they would be accepted, but in every tree they perched, the other birds stared at Bluesky and soon ostracized the entire family.

No bird dared play with Songjoy or Cloudshadow. They wouldn't even think about playing with Bluesky.

A terrible loneliness haunted the bird family.

They saw the other birds in trees and branches nearby, but not one would sing out to them in friendship or association. It felt as if the little family were completely isolated from the rest of the world.

Songjoy, Cloudshadow, and Bluesky felt it too, but they were afraid to mention it to their parents. The young birds could see the same feeling of rejection in the eyes of their parents, and if somehow they missed the sadness and stress in their parents' eyes, there was no way they could ignore the terrible arguments that erupted every night between Treetop and Sunshine.

It scared Bluesky.

He didn't like to hear his mother and father scream at each other. He cried sometimes when they fought. Of course, they tried to hide it from the youngsters. Treetop and Sunshine would fly high up in the tree when their emotions boiled over so the fledglings wouldn't hear their angry words.

Little did they realize that their voices and angry words carried on the breeze; their babies often heard every word.

Bluesky quickly realized that these arguments focused on one main fact -- his parents felt the sting of the ostracism even more than he did.

Treetop was especially angry and took his frustration out on his mate. Unfortunately, Sunshine reciprocated and unleashed her own bitterness right back at him.

A terrible cycle began. Almost every evening Treetop and Sunshine flew off to argue. When they returned, the fledglings still felt the tension that filled the air between their parents.

The peace of the little bird family crumbled little by little as the days of lonely isolation stretched on…

Bluesky knew it was all his fault. He knew the other birds didn't like him, but he now felt his parents' arguing was his fault as well. If it weren't for him, the other birds would accept the rest of his family. He'd guessed it before, but now he knew it… because he'd heard his father shout those very words to his mother.

Bluesky felt terrible inside. He felt so empty and sad.

One evening, as stars slowly appeared in the clear sky above the tree in which they roosted alone, Bluesky noticed his parents hurry off to the topmost branches. Somehow he knew the weeks of anger and distress were coming to a climax. As Cloudshadow and Songjoy went to sleep, he waited until the darkness grew deep and hid the world under its black cloak.

He flew silently up to the top of the tree until the sounds of his parents' angry voices grew discernable.

"*I must leave* -- it's the *only* answer!" Treetop shouted vehemently.

"Breaking up our family can't be the answer!" Sunshine cried.

"What other answer is there? To keep living like this -- isolated from every other bird in the world?"

"We mated for life!" Sunshine whispered sadly.

A terrible silence filled the night.

"Let's try to think this through, shall we?" Treetop's voice grew calm.

"I'm listening."

"You see how every bird treats us -- and it's not just us. Songjoy and Cloudshadow are treated the same way. Not a single bird plays with them or even sings out to them. They'll never learn any social skills. They'll never find a place to live and raise a family of their own." Treetop raised himself up and spoke with sudden clarity. "How will they even find a mate when it's time?"

Another silence, a different silence, now filled the darkness, but as Bluesky strained to hear, a new sound gradually grew louder. Bluesky's heart broke in two when he realized his mother was crying.

"Listen, a lot of birds mate just for one season."

Treetop's tone changed again. His voice was now emotionless and curt. "It doesn't mean the end for us as a mated pair. I'll find you again next spring -- or next summer." His unexpected pause filled Bluesky with uncertainty. Treetop spoke the next words rapidly, searching for conviction.

"We'll raise another family then, just like before…"

"What about the babies we have now? They still need us; they're not ready to fly off on their own."

"I'll take Songjoy and Cloudshadow with me. I'll make sure they prepare for the winter, and I'll find us a place with birds that will accept us and take us in. They'll meet other birds and make friends and begin to live a normal life…"

"What about me?" Sunshine's voice cracked with emotion, filled with bitter resentment. "What about your other baby -- Bluesky? What happens to us?"

"I don't know."

"*You're just going to leave us?*"

"I'll send for you later."

"No, you won't!"

"Songjoy and Cloudshadow deserve a normal life!" Treetop shouted. "We can't give it to them, not like this."

"Not with Bluesky, that's what you really mean."

"You see how the other birds look at him. They think he's a monster, a cripple, a… a…"

"I don't care what other birds say or think."

Sunshine sighed sadly.

"We can't go on living like this."

"We can all go away together. We can fly far away where nobody knows us."

"It won't make any difference. They'll treat us the same -- they'll avoid us and laugh at us. As soon as they see --"

"You don't know that for certain."

"Look at him, Sunshine. *He is different*."

"We can't blame all of this on that poor baby! It's not his fault he was born like that!"

"I've got to leave."

Another tense silence filled the air.

Bluesky stifled a sob as he sat on the branch alone in the dark. After a few moments, he flew back down to the branch where Songjoy and Cloudshadow continued to sleep undisturbed. He envied them their peaceful slumber.

Even after he heard his parents land nearby and settle down, Bluesky's troubled mind would not let him rest, much less drift into sleep. Long into the night, Bluesky sat off to himself on the branch, feeling even more alone than he ever had before.

The next day, Treetop led his family to a new tree, but once again, the other birds avoided any contact with Bluesky or the others.

Bluesky felt so empty inside. He felt so ashamed. He felt so terrible.

When he caught his father looking at him, he turned away quickly. He couldn't look his father in the eyes now.

He noticed a change in his dad too. Treetop

seemed distant, even when they perched side by side on a branch. Bluesky didn't say much to him -- he didn't know what to say any more.

It seemed his father was so sad inside. It seemed his father carried some heavy, invisible weight that bowed him down, crushed him, and tainted his every moment.

It was a terrible weight his father carried.

Bluesky couldn't see it, but he could feel it.

He wished sometime that his father would sing again -- sing like he had the first days after they hatched. His father had been so happy then. Treetop used to sing every day back then -- perched in the highest branch and on the tallest tree.

Bluesky and his brother and sister had learned quickly that Treetop was an excellent singer. Many times their father had lifted his voice in song, his crystal-clear whistles and twinkling trills drawing the rapturous attention of birds both near and far.

It was true that oftentimes a nearby mockingbird, upon hearing another of his kind sing out, would sing out in return. The birds would endeavor to outsing each other in an adult version of the 'Singing Game.' Sometime the other bird would sing back simply out of admiration, imitating the original singer. The two birds might sing in this duet of mutual admiration for many song-filled minutes.

Mockingbirds, however, took the 'Singing Game' much more seriously than other birds -- and if two mockingbirds challenged each other, it was time to watch out! One or both birds might become so excited that they'd pour forth with every phrase, every song, every snippet of song in their entire repertoire in an effort to overwhelm the other. If both mockingbirds were well matched, neither bird might repeat themselves for ten minutes or more at a time. When they really got wound up, two mockingbirds in the midst of the 'Singing Game' were a sight to behold and a delight to hear.

The 'Singing Game' was pervasive throughout the world of birds. Whenever any bird called out or sang, somewhere in the near distance another of its kind would likely sing back.

All birds played the game, but the mockingbird *owned* the 'Singing Game.'

Why?

First, the mocker would play the game with other birds whereas most birds only played with others of their own kind. Second, the mockingbird's never-ending persistence and boundless energy was world renowned, especially when it came to singing. It was a rare bird indeed who defeated a mockingbird in a serious match of the 'Singing Game', and most dared not answer his challenge in the first place.

If a bird did answer a Mockingbird and played the game, it usually was not with the idea of defeating him but simply for the joy of playing.

Yes, the fun was in the playing -- or in this case, the singing.

Birds enjoyed this game so much that they would even play it with humans. When a human whistled in reply to any bird, the bird would most likely sing back and play the game, but if a human dared try to play the game with a Mockingbird ... The moment a mockingbird realized it was a human trying to play, the bird would become even more excitable than if he were playing with another mockingbird. The bird would suddenly redouble his efforts in an attempt to overwhelm the pretender with his innate natural ability and extensive repertoire. Mockingbirds absolutely refused to be beaten at their own game, especially by a mere human.

Bluesky's father used to love the 'Singing Game', but Treetop rarely sang at all now.

"Dad, why don't you sing anymore? I love to hear you sing." Bluesky cocked his long tail expectantly.

"No one wants to sing back, Bluesky. No one wants to join me. It's... it's too lonely to sing by yourself."

"I'll sing with you."

Treetop looked down at Bluesky, and for a fraction of a second it seemed to Bluesky that his father almost opened his beak in a smile. Instead, he sighed very sadly.

"Please sing, Daddy," Songjoy pleaded as she flew up to them and sat on the branch with Treetop and Bluesky.

"I hear other birds singing out from the trees around us," Cloudshadow said. "The birds here seem like friendly kinds of birds. Maybe they'll sing with us."

Sunshine hopped down from a branch above

them. "Try it, Treetop. Surely, some of these birds will see that we are just normal birds like them."

They all looked hopefully at Treetop.

"Sure, I'll sing."

They all broke out in a chorus of chirps and cheers.

"Hush, hush. Let me fly up and find a good spot. Then, I'll need a few moments to get in the mood." He wagged his long tail up and down a moment as he hopped from branch to branch up toward the top. He paused a moment on a branch. Finally, he looked back down at them.

"I will sing a happy song. I'll sing such a song that the other birds will just have to join in. Maybe these birds will accept us."

Bluesky watched his dad with a sense of pride. He knew his father would do it. He would sing, and the other birds wouldn't be able to ignore them any longer. They'd finally find a place where they could live in peace with the other birds.

Treetop finally reached the topmost branch. He looked around at all the birds flying about their business and flitting from tree to tree. With his head lifted toward the sky, he cocked his tail down at an angle and opened his beak wide. Treetop sang forth with all his might, every fiber of his body focused on singing.

He sang out with his favorite melody.

And as the last note echoed on the wind, he added a cheerful little trill just for effect.

Again and again he repeated his song. Each time, his whistles and trills sent a thrill of excitement through Bluesky and Songjoy and Cloudshadow -- and especially Sunshine, but though he sang with all his heart and in the clearest of voice and with the happiest of songs, no one answered in reply.

He sang harder and louder. His chirps and tuneful twitters and wonderful warbles increased tenfold, but still, not a single bird called back either in challenge or appreciation.

Still he sang, more loudly and with even more melodic trills. He wouldn't give up.

Treetop sang so sweetly that even in trees hidden from view birds sat up and listened attentively. After a few moments, many of them took wing and flew toward the source of the magnificent singer.

Bluesky knew exactly what his father was doing. He saw a mockingbird suddenly land a branch below his father and look up at Treetop. Seconds later, a towhee and then a robin appeared in other branches, each looking up toward the happy singer.

Bluesky tried to hide in the shadows of the leaves so the birds wouldn't see him, but the more he tried to be unobtrusive, the more the whispers and stares found him out.

He saw birds land in the branches of this tree and the others nearby, drawn by Treetop's voice, but instead of joining his father in song, they stared in critical silence at him.

Although a growing number of birds flew toward Treetop's pleasant songs, the moment they spotted the little one-legged bird hiding among the shadows, they whispered among themselves and took flight as quickly as they had come.

"Sing, Father! Keep singing!" Songjoy cried out as her father paused. Cloudshadow suddenly burst out in perfect imitation of Treetop's melody. Sunshine echoed her own variation in an effort to prompt other birds to join.

Finally, Bluesky lifted his voice in support. As his last note echoed on the breeze, Bluesky looked up at his father.

Treetop stared without emotion down at him, but he did not sing back in reply.

With great sadness, Bluesky watched as his father took wing and flew off alone.

"Where are you going, Dad?" Bluesky cried out.

"I need to be alone for a while. I need some time... I need to think."

As Bluesky watched him leave, his heart sank.

"Where's Dad going?" Bluesky asked his mother when she hopped down beside him.

"I don't know, little one. Don't worry. Let's go find a nice branch where we can all perch for the night."

Bluesky couldn't help but worry. Again, a great emptiness smothered his heart with sadness.

It was his fault. If it weren't for him, his dad would be happy. If it weren't for him, other birds would join him in song. If it weren't for him, the other birds would accept his parents and his siblings.

He again had trouble falling asleep that night. His mind rambled with troubled thoughts a long, long time until it seemed sleep would never come, but somewhere in the night, time seemed to slow and grow meaningless, and blissful sleep finally quieted all his fears.

Bluesky awakened with the first birdsongs as the eastern sky brightened. He looked around the branch. He saw his mother a short distance away.

Suddenly, his heart began to race and his head grew faint.

"Where's Songjoy, Mom?" Bluesky cried out in fear. "And Cloudshadow, and... and Dad!" Bluesky hopped over to Sunshine and pushed his body close to her. He felt the comforting warmth of her feathers, but the rapid beating of his heart and the chilling panic continued to fill him with fear.

"Where are they, Mom?" Bluesky pleaded with tears in his eyes.

"They're gone." Sunshine lowered her head while her sadness fell out of her eyes as tears.

"We've got to find them!"

Sunshine wrapped a wing around Bluesky's back. "It's just you and I, Bluesky. We'll have to look out for each other now."

"But..." Bluesky's body shook with emotion. His voice failed him; his mind was gripped with fear and shock and sadness.

"But... I didn't even get to tell them good-bye!"

Sunshine breathed in deeply, her eyes moist with tears.

"We'll see them again after the winter, Bluesky.

When the flowers bloom again and the trees grow new leaves."

"I can't believe they're… gone!"

"I woke up just like you a few moments ago and found them gone. I can't believe it either."

"Where did they go?" Bluesky cried again.

"I don't know. I wish I did."

"Can we find them?"

"I don't know where to look."

Bluesky cried out with a mournful, forlorn whistle.

"Please, don't cry baby." Sunshine wrapped her wing tighter around Bluesky's back.

"I'm afraid, Mom."

"I'm a little afraid too. We'll have to take care of each other."

Bluesky looked up at his mother and peered deeply into her eyes. "You won't leave me, will you, Mom?"

Sunshine leaned over and rubbed her long, curved beak comfortingly over Bluesky's head and the back of his neck. Again and again she caressed him with loving strokes. Finally, she whispered with calm assurance into his ear, "I will never leave you."

"Do you promise?" Bluesky asked fearfully.

"I promise."

223

Chapter Seventeen

Bluesky and Sunshine.

The two mockingbirds were inseparable. Where one ate, the other was nearby. Where one sat on a tree and sang, the other was within earshot and usually joined in the song. And where one flew in the sky, the other was not far away.

They were always together.

Sunshine loved her baby bird and tried to give him everything he needed, and Bluesky loved his mother with a boundless joy. Their entire world revolved around each other now.

True, the first days and weeks after his father and siblings left were difficult. Bluesky had been lonely before, but now it seemed his only friend in the entire world was his mother.

Bluesky thought of them often. He missed them terribly, but if he mentioned any of them by name, his mother's eyes filled with tears, and Bluesky could not bear to see his mother cry.

He no longer mentioned them in conversation now, and that made his sadness even deeper.

Bluesky learned a new trait. He learned to ignore the stares and whispers of the other birds. He even learned to ignore how the other mockingbirds shunned him and his mother.

He didn't need them anyway. He only needed Sunshine.

Bluesky didn't realize how much the sudden departure of his father affected him at first, but after a few days of living with just his mother as a companion, he experienced frightening nightmares.

Most of his sleep was pleasant and refreshing as it should be, but sometimes as the night sky just began to lighten, his sleep would become troubled and filled with fear. In his nightmares every bird suddenly disappeared. He would fly as high and as far as his wings would allow, but the world around him was empty of all birds -- except for him. As his fear rose to a panic-filled crescendo, he'd realize he was totally alone in the entire world!

Even his mother was gone!

He always awakened from this nightmare with a start and with his heart pounding inside his chest. The first thing he always did was search for his mother's familiar form. Once he spotted her on a nearby branch, he'd quickly hop right up beside her and lean against her for reassurance.

The comfort of her presence meant everything to him after those awful nightmares.

Much to his dismay, the nightmare recurred more and more often.

The dog days of summer arrived. Every living thing -- birds, animals and people -- sweltered under the heat of the sun combined with the high humidity. Days were now a time to hide in the cool shade of the great trees and focus on meals in the morning and early evenings when the harsh sun was low in the sky.

Surprisingly to Bluesky, because he had never experienced autumn, and not at all unwelcome, the dog days were soon replaced with more moderate temperatures and lower humidity as autumn approached. Gray clouds and a fresh west wind heralded the first cold front from Canada. The front swept through Georgia, bringing with it the refreshingly cool, clean air from the far north.

The end of summer was near, and soon the mornings dawned with a chill in the air as more cold fronts swept down.

For the first time in his life, Bluesky observed the deep green leaves of the trees change into a rainbow of colors -- untold shades of orange, red, and brown. After the first frost of the year, the colorful leaves filled the trees with a riotous display of autumn color.

Bluesky experienced his first taste of cold weather.

His mother urged him to eat more in preparation for winter's cruel onslaught. Bluesky obeyed and ate twice as much as he had before, and yet, although he put on added weight and fat for protection, he would notice his mother standing idly off to the side. He soon realized she was eating less, but when he asked her why she wasn't eating, she'd simply shake her head and stare off into the distance with sadness in her eyes.

Her silent sadness worried Bluesky, but he had no idea how to help her.

When the nights suddenly became uncomfortably cold, he wasn't quite sure if he liked this change in the air now. However, very soon Bluesky realized the colder air was thicker and heavier than the warm air of summer. Even better, when the cool air collided with the warm air, it created fabulous winds and breezes that made flying that much better.

And flying was Bluesky's favorite thing.

He'd leave his mother snoozing in a tree and fly off by himself most times. While he flew above the tops of the trees with the cool air in his face and the warmth of the sun on his back, it made him forget all his troubles. He just flew.

Looking down at the islands of treetops and the patchwork of land below, he felt such wonderful freedom. He felt so alive!

And with his heart and soul filled with joy, he felt an urgent need to perch on a high branch and give voice to his burning emotions in song. No bird ever sang back in reply, but it didn't matter to Bluesky. He was happy, and he sang it out for the world to hear.

One evening, as the cold air of autumn chilled the evening air, Bluesky hopped up next to Sunshine where she sat on a branch of a big pine tree. "Mama, will I ever make friends with other birds?"

Sunshine looked down at him with a twinkle of love in her eyes. "I think you will one day, baby."

Bluesky looked down with a forlorn expression. "But no bird will play with me, and no one will sing back to me when I sing."

Sunshine wrapped her wing around his back and comforted him. "One day they will -- I just know it."

Bluesky looked up at her with hope as he

nestled deeper into her warm embrace. "How do you know that, Mama?"

"Well, it's long been said among birds -- 'Say good things about others, and they'll say good things about you. Do good things for others, and they'll do good things for you. Treat others like a friend, and soon you will have lots of friends.'"

"I try to be nice to other birds, Mama, but they always fly away." Bluesky started to cry softly.

Sunshine tightened her embrace around Bluesky. "One day, birds will see beyond the fact you only have one leg. They'll look beyond your outer appearance and see what kind of bird you are on the inside -- inside your heart."

"How will they do that, Mama?"

She opened her beak and smiled at his questioning eyes. "They'll see that you're a good bird, and they will realize that where it counts, you are just like them too."

"Are all birds good?"

Sunshine paused a moment, looking up at the auburn sky while the last rays of the sun disappeared.

"There is good in all birds. If you look for the good, you'll find it, but if you look for the bad, you'll find it as well."

"I don't understand, Mama."

"You will when you get bigger." She leaned over and caressed his head with her beak. "Always remember this, Bluesky. Always look for the good in other birds. You won't realize it at first, but it'll make you a happier bird."

"You're smart, Mama." Bluesky smiled up at her.

"No, not as smart as you think."

"Tell me a Song-Tale, Mama. Please! You promised you'd tell us about Merryday and Eveningsky."

Sunshine choked back a sob as she turned her head away from Bluesky.

"What's the matter? Did I say something wrong?"

"I-I don't feel like singing a love tale tonight. It's such a long tale too."

"What about Skysinger, the greatest singer ever?"

"That's a long one too, but…" She patted him on the head when she saw the look of disappointment crossing his face. "I'll tell you what. I'll sing the original song of Skysinger that was sung around the world that first time -- and what's more, I'll teach you how to sing it."

"Do mothers always teach their babies a song?" Bluesky asked excitedly.

"Most mothers teach their babies a song -- something special that they'll always share together their entire lives. Tonight, I'll teach you the song of Skysinger."

Sunshine sang the song of Skysinger with a voice full of emotion. As Bluesky listened to the music and words, he quickly realized why the song touched the hearts of the birds all those years ago and why they repeated it again and again until it was sung around the world.

229

She finished it so suddenly that Bluesky thought there must be more.

"Of course there's more, but the entire Song-Tale couldn't have been sung around the world. Now, listen closely and sing after with me."

And so Sunshine taught Bluesky the song of Skysinger...

***

Skysinger, sing!
Songs more beautiful than all others.
All who heard him listened with awe.
No bird ever heard a more happy sound,
Every bird sang back to Skysinger,
And all shared the joy of his song...

But Skysinger grew proud;
He knew he was the best.
Soon he sang for himself alone.
He still sang beautifully, but pride killed the joy.
The birds still heard the greatest singer of all,
But now all flew away.
Skysinger sang alone, the saddest song of all.

One day Skysinger found a robin so very sick.
Skysinger helped him, he even fed him,
But Morninglaughter grew worse.
Farewell, Skysinger. I must die.
My very soul is stricken,
With no hope to keep me breathing,
And no joy to keep my heart beating.

Bluesky and Sunshine

Let me die…
Skysinger mourned his only friend.
But he would not let go.
Skysinger sang just for him.
He sang to reach the heart.
Songs of love, and laughter, and life
Morninglaughter listened to the golden-voiced bird.

The robin grew stronger with the healing of song.
Skysinger sang even more,
But not for himself, and not for pride.
He sang to give.
Morninglaughter's hope and joy returned.
He recovered and joined his friend in song.
Skysinger sang as beautifully as before.
But now he sang to share his joy,
And soon all birds were again his friends.

***

After the fifth time singing the entire song, Sunshine slowly let her voice fade under Bluesky's voice until Bluesky sang the song on his own. Bluesky sang happily, singing the Song-Tale of Skysinger. As Bluesky finished the last note, his mother bent over and kissed him on top of his head.

"No matter where you go or how long you live, when you sing this song think of me, and you must tell every bird you meet -- *this is the song my mother taught me*."

"I will always remember, Mama!" Bluesky chirped happily.

Chapter Eighteen

Winter came early to Georgia.

First one and then another wave of cold arctic air blew down from the far north and evaporated the warm air completely.

For the first time in his life, Bluesky shivered.

The wind was now their enemy. Bitterly cold winds sucked the warmth out of his body until he found himself shaking all over. Bluesky quickly realized he didn't like winter, and he especially hated the cold, dark nights.

During the first cold spell, just before the first hard frost, Bluesky and Sunshine received an unexpected visitor.

"Uncle Seawind!" Sunshine shouted with unabashed happiness as she recognized her dear relative.

"Well, hello there, Sunshine. I haven't seen you this entire season." The old mockingbird hopped closer.

"Yes, I think the last time we met was this time last year when the first cold air arrived. You were telling us you were bound and determined to fly back to the ocean and live out your last days beside it." Sunshine's eyes sparkled with joy.

Bluesky hopped over next to his mother.

Uncle Seawind peered down at Bluesky. "Why don't you use your other leg, young fella? Don't you think it would make hopping easier?"

Bluesky looked down in embarrassment.

"Uncle, Bluesky only has one leg." Sunshine's demeanor changed with her words, almost as if she expected Uncle Seawind to fly off immediately.

"Is that right?" he said with sudden interest. "I never heard of a one-legged mockingbird before." He peered hard at Bluesky's missing leg.

"Never mind that -- how have you been, Uncle? Are you ready to move down by the warm waters of the sea again?"

Seawind chuckled in response. "Yes, yes, I know. Everyone makes fun of me because of that, and I know I'm always talking about flying back to where I was born, but this year I'm finally going to do it. In fact, I'm flying south right now."

He opened his beak in a wide smile. "I'm really going to do it this time!"

"Good for you, Uncle!" Sunshine smiled in return.

Uncle Seawind suddenly took a renewed interest and looked Sunshine up and down as he had when he first greeted her. "Now, Sunshine. You've lost weight, gal. You're too skinny for sure. Ain't no time for that with winter coming. Are you sick or something?"

"I-I haven't been sleeping well. Not... for a while now." Sunshine coughed nervously.

The three sat in awkward silence a moment until Bluesky spoke up. "Did you grow up by the ocean? Did you live there?" Bluesky's eager questions diverted Seawind's attention away from Sunshine.

"Why, I sure did, little fella. Best days of my life, let me tell ya."

233

"Oh! Tell me about them. Did you see any pelicans?"

"Why, sure I did. I met one named Waveglider."

Seawind proceeded to recount his first seasons of life when he lived by the seashore on Tybee Island. It became quickly evident that the old bird lived in the past. He spoke of his early days with an intensity and yearning that belied his years.

After Seawind swooped down for some bugs, Sunshine explained to Bluesky that Uncle Seawind was considered a bit of an eccentric by the rest of the family. He had flown up several seasons ago to meet his cousins and somehow never returned home, and yet all he ever talked about was his early life back beside the sea and going back -- even the first day he arrived.

Uncle Seawind could talk for hours and hours and not let another bird get a word in edgewise. Bluesky assumed that was why many considered him a bit of an odd bird, but Bluesky enjoyed his stories and listened all evening as Seawind told him of his life near the sea.

It sounded like a wonderful place, and although the summers were long and hot and humid, the winters were mild and pleasant.

Seawind told him about all the birds that lived there -- pelicans and seagulls, tiny terns, and all manner of heron and egrets. Bluesky wondered what the forests looked like with their branches draped in soft, flowing blankets of Spanish moss.

Bluesky also tried to imagine, solely on Uncle's

grand descriptions, what palm trees looked like -- tall trees devoid of branches and leaves except at their very top, and with leaves that were exotic and fan-like in shape. He also heard for the first time about palmetto trees, cypress trees, and live oaks. He was especially intrigued by live oaks, a tree whose leaves stayed green all year long.

Late that evening, despite Uncle Seawind's nonstop stories of long ago, Bluesky's eyes grew heavy, and he finally fell asleep. He dreamed of the ocean with squadrons of pelicans flying over the water and long lines of palmetto trees.

Bluesky enjoyed the next few days immensely. He hadn't realized how lonely he and his mother had been until the old bird showed up. They spent the days in constant conversation -- well, Bluesky and Sunshine mostly listened while Uncle Seawind did the conversing. Still, it felt good to have someone else around.

He sensed his mother's inner happiness too. She seemed happier. Bluesky wasn't quite sure how he knew it, but he knew it. Perhaps it was the way her eyes sparkled as she listened intently to Uncle Seawind. Or perhaps it was the way she laughed at his jokes, although she admitted to Bluesky in confidence that she had heard them all before.

At times, though, Bluesky would land on a tree branch and still find his mother perched in silent solitude staring off into the distance. It seemed at those times that she was waiting expectantly for something -- or someone.

Uncle Seawind had even picked up on it after a while, in spite of his almost non-stop verbal assault, but Sunshine never told him who she was waiting for.

The nights grew colder with the passing of each day. Indeed, the days themselves were growing noticeably shorter and shorter with each passage of the sun through the sky.

Sadly, the day came when Seawind decided it was time to fly south.

"*There's a time to fly north, and there's a time to fly south.*" Seawind winked at Bluesky. "I guess you've heard that one before, eh, birdy?"

"Uh, no. That's the first time I've heard that proverb." Bluesky shrugged with noticeable embarrassment.

"What?" Seawind said in disbelief. "You mean I've finally said something to someone they haven't heard from me before!" The old mockingbird laughed at himself in sheer delight. "I know I talk too much, but well, I just love to talk! That's all there is to it." He laughed again.

"Why don't you spend the winter with us, Uncle. We'd love to have you. Wouldn't we, Bluesky?" Sunshine's voice had a powerful, yet subtle urgency.

"Oh no, no, no. It wouldn't do. I've been saying for all these years that I need to fly back to the sea and get away from these cold winters around here. I'm getting too old for this."

Sunshine bowed her head and let out a soft sigh.

"Now, now, my pretty little mockingbird. You

aren't the same bird I once knew. You used to smile and laugh all the time, and you're not eating enough. You've got to build yourself up." Seawind tapped her on the shoulder with his wingtip. "I hear winter is going to be brutally cold this year. That's why I'm going now. I should have left a month ago."

"I, I just wish you'd stay with us. We... we really enjoyed your company these past few days. You don't know how much it's meant to us." Sunshine's eyes pleaded to Seawind even more than her words.

Seawind paused in silence a moment -- totally out of character. He studied Sunshine and then looked deep into her eyes. "What's the matter, Sunshine? You're not physically sick, I don't think, but this sickness you have -- it's a sickness of the heart. Yes..."

Sunshine didn't reply.

The three birds flew together and ate some more, but now even Seawind remained mostly silent. In the end, he hopped up suddenly as the sun began to set low in the western sky.

"I'm leaving now. Why don't you two go with me?"

"I-I can't go." Sunshine turned away from him.

"Why can't we, Mama? I'd love to go see the ocean and the pelicans. We could fly back in the spring... or the summer." Bluesky hopped up and down excitedly.

"What..." Sunshine paused. "What if your father comes looking for us, and we're not here?"

Bluesky contemplated her words with a deep and serious attitude.

Before he could reply, Sunshine continued, "I'm sorry, Uncle. I wish we could, but we can't leave, not just now."

Seawind nodded with understanding. "I hope I see you again soon, my dear. I've really enjoyed these last few days with you two." Seawind smiled at Sunshine and Bluesky.

Bluesky was sad to see the old bird leave -- deeply saddened.

Now, it was just he and his mother again.

His mother chided him every day, constantly urging him to eat and keep up his strength, but he noticed every day how little his mother ate and how it seemed she was so sad inside.

It made him sad to realize something troubled her so deeply, but being young, he didn't know what to do or say except to be obedient and do as he was told.

He hoped that somehow he could make his mother happier by obeying her. He wished it with all his heart.

After one of the warmest days they'd experienced in many weeks, Bluesky noticed an impending change. He didn't know it, but a major cold front bringing freezing, sub-arctic air was making it way south with bone-chilling suddenness.

Gray clouds filled the northwestern sky as the Artic Clipper swept southward, bringing with it a drop in temperature to chill the very soul.

It had almost felt like spring that day, the sun

shone so brightly and filled the world with warmth, but the cold air would drop the temperature far below freezing that very night -- a terrible and sudden change. The worst part would be the brutal winds.

"Bluesky, we've got to find a shelter."

Bluesky looked up at his mama. "Why, Mama? It was so warm today."

A strong breeze ruffled her feathers as she fought to maintain her balance. "There's a cold front coming with very cold air, and strong winds. This is air from the top of the world -- *a killing cold*. We need to find a tree that will protect us from the wind."

"Okay, Mama." Bluesky looked around. "Which tree?"

"I... don't know. Treetop was always so good at picking..." Sunshine shuddered as a blast of freezing air swirled around them.

Bluesky shivered with the cold air that pierced through his feathers and chilled his body. "I don't like this cold wind, Mama. It makes me shake."

Sunshine sneezed.

"Do you have a cold, Mama?"

"No, no. It's just this wind. C'mon, let's try the old oak tree. It has such a huge trunk and many branches; surely we can find protection there."

But there was no room for them, and the birds already roosting there turned a cold shoulder to their inquiries. They ordered Sunshine and Bluesky to find another tree.

The key to survival was to stay warm, and the

biggest issue was getting out of the direct wind. As the stars grew in the sky, the wind grew stronger and stronger and the temperature dropped precipitously.

The drastic change in temperature was mind numbing, and for any creature dwelling out of doors, it was dangerous.

Sunshine told Bluesky how to fluff his feathers out and hold his body still in order to conserve body heat. She repeated to him over and over how important this would be tonight with the strong winds and cold air sweeping down upon them.

Bluesky felt he must have made his mother mad somehow. She kept repeating herself, and she seemed out of sorts. She seemed so upset. He felt for certain he had done something wrong, but he didn't know what.

As the night grew dark, darker than he had ever experienced before, Bluesky peered toward his mother on a branch just below him. She shivered in the cold wind, her feathers blown and her body wobbling as she fought for balance. Once again, she chided him for not keeping his feathers fluffed out.

"I'm doing my best, Mama." Bluesky said sheepishly. He hung his head and tried to keep from crying.

"It's all right, baby. You're doing good. I'm just worried about you -- that's all. It's so cold tonight... I can't seem to keep myself warm. I just..." She paused. "I'm worried about you."

"I'll keep warm, Mama. I'm just having trouble

perching here. The wind keeps pushing me!"

"Hold tight, Bluesky."

Bluesky couldn't see her now through the darkness, but he could sense her loving gaze.

"You're my good baby, Bluesky. I'm -- I'm so proud of you."

Bluesky didn't know what to say in reply, and just then, a powerful blast of wind sent a wave of frigid air inside his protective shield of feathers and chilled him until he shivered and shook like a leaf on a tree. He tried to fluff out his feathers better after the wind subsided.

"I'm so... so very proud of you." Sunshine's voice whispered on the wind.

The wind howled and wailed as though a thousand birds cried out all at once.

Bluesky clenched his eyes shut and concentrated with all his might. It was hard for him. He perched low on the branch, gripping the bark with his one foot, but the wind was relentless. All night long he battled, concentrating on keeping his feathers fluffed just right and also trying to keep his balance. A hundred times during the night, when the wind howled and roared and the temperature continued falling, Bluesky felt the cold take his breath away as it penetrated his feathers again and again. It was real work. It took all his strength to keep from being swept off the branch and into the darkness.

He didn't try to speak to his mother any more. He was too tired. He had to stay warm.

He fought to stay warm.

He fought to stay alive.

He wished his mother was beside him, so they could try to keep warm together. But the branch was so small there wasn't room for both of them. Where he sat, the slender trunk of this small tree kept the worst of the wind off. His mother had found a different branch to help fend off the wicked wind for her.

Alone in the dark, each huddled alone against the killing cold.

He knew his mother worried about him, and he didn't want her to worry. He feared that was the source of her deep and unspoken sadness. If he had been a season older, he would have realized it was her broken heart, the loss of her mate, that distressed her and consumed her.

The terrible cold and the brutal winds grew more intense as the night grew darker. The howling of the wind seemed to punctuate the misery every creature felt. Every creature trapped in its freezing grasp sought shelter, any kind of shelter, and protection from its life-sapping fury.

Somewhere in the deep, dark night, Sunshine faded away...

The wind rose to a wailing crescendo. In the midst of the frozen night, the invisible power seemingly lifted the still and silent mockingbird off the branch. Sunshine fell down into the darkness until she disappeared into a pile of leaves.

The night and the wind and the cold seemed to last forever.

Somewhere in the wee hours, Bluesky fell into a fitful sleep filled with nightmares. A part of his mind continued to concentrate on his balance and his protective feathers. Maybe it was instinct; maybe it was his mother's words. It was probably both.

Just before the black night began to lighten in the east, his familiar nightmare returned.

He was alone -- utterly alone.

And no one cared for him...

Bluesky awoke with a start from his all-too-familiar nightmare.

"Mama!" he cried out.

He looked down at the branch where she perched last night, but she wasn't there!

"MAMA!" Bluesky shouted in sheer panic.

He hopped down to where he last saw her and searched frantically up and down the entire length of the branch. Fear gripped his mind in an iron vise. With a flash of feathers, he flew through the trees calling out desperately a single word over and over and over again.

"Mama!"

He searched for her everywhere.

Bluesky didn't notice the sun rise over the trees. The clean air from the arctic made the day seem different -- everything was clear and cold.

But not to Bluesky.

Everything was confusion and fear for him. He barely noticed the world. All he could focus upon was finding his mother. That one thought burned inside his mind.

As the sun soared high in the sky, Bluesky continued to search. In fact, his search grew more intense and more desperate.

The other birds who had survived the freezing winds sang out with the joy of living another day. The morning chorus had not started in earnest with the rising of the winter sun. No, the birds slowly grew to activity while the frozen air warmed around them. Only after the sun was well on its daily journey through the sky did the birds begin to sing out loud this winter day, but once their songs began, there was no ignoring them.

Bluesky did not hear them.

He flew from tree to tree, calling out in desperation, but his mother did not answer.

He flew high into the sky and looked all around for any sign of her.

He never felt his hunger, even long past the time he should have eaten many times that day. No, all the little one-legged mockingbird felt was his all-consuming fear.

The sun finally warmed the world and everything in its sight by late in the afternoon.

Many creatures had succumbed to the sudden freeze the night before. If Bluesky had noticed, he would have seen other creatures lying frozen in the shadows, but he only had eyes for his mother.

As the sun started to lower into the west, an idea grew inside his consciousness. He knew the reason, the real reason, why he'd awoken alone.

His mother had left him. She had broken her promise.

But he understood why now! She had left him to go and find his father and siblings. Yes, that was

244

why she had abandoned him.

He knew where to go now.

Bluesky flew to the ancient oak tree whose branches held countless birds at any one time. He landed on a branch where a familiar mockingbird perched.

"Aunty Coldrain! Aunty Coldrain!" Bluesky shouted breathlessly.

Coldrain stared at him in shocked surprise. "What? What are *you* doing here?" She gazed at down at him with a cold, condescending glare.

"I-I can't find my mama! I have to find her!"

"You're kidding! You mean she's left you too, just like your father and your siblings?" Coldrain's eyes remained emotionless.

Bluesky's spirit was crushed by her cruel words. He looked down, defeated and heart-broken.

"Well, I can't blame her, you know..."

Bluesky couldn't listen to any more. He flew off with a flash of feathers, but now he no longer had the strength to call out for his mother. In fact, he felt it a useless gesture -- she would not answer him. She'd left him on purpose, and Aunt Coldrain had confirmed his deepest fear: he was alone, utterly alone.

He flew blindly.

Bluesky flew on and on, not really knowing where he was going, and he no longer cared. It didn't really matter.

"Hey, one-legged bird! Where are you flying to so fast?"

Bluesky turned to see another mockingbird

flying toward him.

It was Funwind. "What's the matter, one-legged bird? You look like you've lost your last friend in the whole world!" Funwind taunted with heartless cruelty.

"Leave me alone!" Bluesky shouted with despair. He turned away, hiding the tears in his eyes. "Just leave me alone!"

"Ah, poor little bird... Nobody likes you. Nobody likes a weird, one-legged bird like you."

Bluesky flapped his wings faster and faster. He flew faster than the wind. He felt he must, in order to escape the taunts of Funwind, but more importantly, he suddenly felt the strange conviction that if he flew fast enough he could even escape the loneliness and pain.

He had to try.

He heard Funwind shouting behind him, but he ignored his words. He flew even faster. He had to escape -- he had to. Or else...

Funwind slowly fell behind and finally turned away, but as Bluesky grew distant, he shouted over his shoulder one last time.

"Stupid bird, you won't outfly me next time."

Bluesky heard him, but he didn't care. His troubled mind grew clouded again.

Somehow, he found himself in the very tree where he and his mother had perched the night before. With a heavy heart, he landed on the branch where he last saw his mother. A faint spark of hope once again burned inside his breast.

Perhaps his mother had only gotten lost? If that

were true, she'd return here, the last place they had been together.

Bluesky mentally kicked himself for having left. He should have stayed here all day and not moved. He was so stupid!

Everything he did was wrong!

He remembered now -- his mother had promised never to leave him. She would never break a promise.

She had probably waited on him here and wondered why he had left her! Oh, Funwind was right. He was nothing but a stupid, stupid bird.

As the sun sank to the horizon, he finally felt the faint pangs of hunger. He suddenly realized he had not eaten a single bite the entire day. His mother would be mad at him for that too, and how would he be able to stay warm tonight?

He needed nourishment, but he was too exhausted to hop down and try to find a bug now.

He was so tired, so very tired. Every muscle in his body ached -- ached with tiredness, ached with sadness, ached with mind-numbing agony.

As the sun slipped below the tree-lined horizon, the fragile warmth of the day evaporated.

And with the growing darkness, the killing cold returned.

Chapter Nineteen

Bluesky would never see his mother or his father again.

The heart-piercing hopelessness of that terrible truth consumed him whole. Overwhelming dread enveloped him with a greater darkness and a more bone-chilling cold than even the frozen air of that dark, winter night.

He was totally alone now.

The real darkness closed tighter as the freezing air took his breath away.

Thousands of stars sparkled like tiny diamonds against the black night. Time had no meaning here; everything seemed to slow down. Confusion filled his mind until the resulting disorientation made him sway as if intoxicated.

A terrible sadness paralyzed his thoughts and suffocated his very being.

And the sadness hurt.

He was all alone in the world.

He had no friends, and now, he had no family.

Nobody loved him.

Nobody cared.

Intense fear seized his heart and gripped it like a steel vise. Indeed, every part of his being ached and screamed with suffering and overwhelming exhaustion. The cold air merely intensified his pain and misery.

The temperature dropped quickly now that the warmth of the sun had disappeared.

It hurt so badly...

The fear that filled him was also sadness. Or was the sadness fear? Both were a terrible darkness, an aching emptiness, an emptiness as huge as the black sky above -- but it was all inside him -- inside his heart. The pain pressed and gripped him tighter and tighter. He ached everywhere; every joint in his body screamed in agony.

Everything was cold and fear and sadness and pain -- and loneliness...

It hurt so badly he felt he must surely die!

Every beat of his heart sent another bolt of pain throughout his being.

As if by instinct Bluesky called out for help; he cried as though threatened by some great danger. His call was but a single note -- a long, drawn-out, and mournful note that rose in intensity and slowly, so very slowly, faded away in utter silence into the darkness.

He cried out for his mother and his father.

He cried out because of his terrible grief.

He wanted so badly to see them just one more time, to talk with them just one more time -- to tell them he loved them just one more time. He wanted to tell them how much they had helped him. He wanted to... just see them one more time and be near them and feel that wonderful comfort that came from just being near them, *but he would never see them again*.

He shivered against the frigid air. The cold grew and seemed to penetrate every part of his body and fuse with the cold inside his heart. He didn't fluff out his feathers to present a layer of protection against the killing cold tonight.

He didn't care anymore.

He didn't care if died.

In fact, he welcomed death. It would mean an end to this awful emptiness that sucked the life out of him and filled him with such bitter pain. It would mean an end to his loneliness.

The dark and the cold grew more intense with each passing minute, and so did Bluesky's sadness.

He couldn't move now; the cold and pain held him in bondage with overwhelming force. All he could manage was to cry out from time to time with that solitary and mournful note that embodied his bitter grief.

Almost against his will, he perched lower in an almost normal position for rest. He didn't deserve the comforting folds of sleep, but the fatigue filled his mind, and it came anyway.

The terrible pain, however, wouldn't let go, and Bluesky closed his eyes as much to flee the pain as to take solace in rest.

The bitterly cold winds continued to blow as the cold front continued to flood farther and farther south. Within the grip of this frigid air, any creature out in the open died after only a few moments of exposure.

Surprisingly, birds were well-equipped to deal with this condition. Their feathers were a natural insulator and buffered the cold air -- preventing it from reaching the body -- while trapping the lifesaving warmth of the body underneath. By fluffing out their feathers, they could make this buffer greater.

Bluesky grew more confused as exhaustion now wrestled with his pain. He had flown all day vainly searching for his mother, not even stopping once to eat. His muscles ached as much from his extensive exertions as from his all-consuming grief.

He drifted into a troubled sleep filled with unseen terrors that reached for him from every direction, and worse, he had nowhere to flee.

He was alone.

Mercifully, the all-consuming pain faded.

And yet, every few minutes the pain and sadness slowly grew again until even his sleeping subconscious became troubled. The pervasive sorrow eventually became so powerful it felt like his heart would explode. Even within of the dark folds of sleep where he should have found some relief, the terrible pain filled his mind and squeezed his heart so hard he couldn't find solace even there. The bitter cold from without and the numbing loneliness from within squeezed him unmercifully in its relentless vise until he cried out.

He couldn't help but cry out again and again as the pressure grew so intense that it hurt. Each mournful cry made Bluesky feel as if a tiny part of himself had died. As each mournful cry slowly faded on the wind, Bluesky fell back into his troubled sleep.

All around Bluesky, other birds and animals wondered at this heart-rending call of sadness, but every animal's one focus was on staying warm this cold night. No animal or bird moved to investigate -- not even a possum or other predator that would normally come and devour any creature who called out like this as if asking to be eaten.

It was too cold to move.

Finally, late into the night, the winds subsided.

Throughout the long, dark night, the silence of the frozen world was complete -- complete except for the mournful wail of a single bird...

Chapter Twenty

Mark was 'on call' that week.

He didn't get paged in the middle of the night very often. His employer's computers and applications were stable, and a strict 'Change Management Process' kept things running smoothly.

He slept deeply under the covers, and the warmth of his wife's back felt so good against his own back. It was almost three o'clock in the morning when his phone buzzed angrily.

He groaned as he reached toward the nightstand, the cold air against his arm making him shiver. He blindly felt for his phone, knocking something unseen off the table and onto the floor before he could find it.

His phone buzzed angrily again.

He groaned again as he switched on the light. He sat up in bed and read the message -- 'OP Support. Pls Logon ASAP Booking application is down.'

The cold air washed over his exposed skin when he threw back the covers; it was freezing even inside the house. They always turned the heat down at night in order to save a little money on the heating bill, but tonight it felt like there was no heat on at all!

Mark shivered, reaching over to the chair beside the bed and quickly grabbing his clothes lying across it. He then jumped out of bed and threw on a shirt, his blue jeans, and his house shoes with rapid-fire motions. He still shivered even after he finished.

It was a penetrating cold this night -- an intensely brutal chill in the air that sucked the warmth from everything.

Mark carefully made it down the stairs and to his computer. He switched on the power and watched the familiar logo flash past on the screen. A few minutes later, he opened an active VPN connection to his company's intranet.

He rubbed his eyes as he tried to clear his mind from the fog of sleep.

The sound of soft footsteps padding on the carpet caused him to turn.

"It's too early for Daddy to be up, eh, Buddy?" Mark said with a yawn.

Buddy peered around the corner and yawned lazily in agreement. Satisfied no stranger had invaded their home, the long-haired cat ambled over to a small throw rug, lay down, and curled himself tightly for warmth.

He faced Mark in order to keep an eye on things.

As Buddy rested his head onto his front paws, KC stuck her head inside the doorway.

"Who's the pretty kitty?"

"Mrrr-oww," KC half-purred and half-meowed.

KC trotted over to Mark and brushed her side against his leg. Mark reached down and caressed her ear lovingly. She purred in delight and arched her back as he caressed her other ear.

Mark looked up at the screen as data rolled across it. He typed some commands.

KC padded across the floor to Buddy. They sniffed each other nose-to-nose, and then, satisfied, they both looked up at Mark with curiosity glowing from their eyes.

Mark smiled back.

KC joined Buddy on the rug as she too curled up for warmth, her tail swishing contentedly.

As he sat before the computer and started reading the information on the screen, a strange and haunting cry echoed from the blackness outside the window. He looked toward the window and noticed the pale moonlight outlining a solitary tree outside.

From the frigid darkness, a grief-stricken cry penetrated the frozen silence.

Both cats looked up, their eyes wide with interest.

Mark stared out the window with a puzzled expression. He knew it was a bird, but he'd never heard a bird make such a terribly sad sound in all his life! He figured the poor bird was cold, but this call sounded as if the bird had given up. Perhaps all the warmth had left its body, and the frigid cold held it in a relentless death-grip?

It sounded like the bird was so miserable it wanted to die.

The sadness of that mournful call touched his heart. He groaned in empathy as he replayed the sad cry inside his mind.

The next moment his body shivered violently, whether from the intense cold or out of compassion

255

for the little creature, he wasn't quite sure.

He slowly shook his head and wrapped his arms around himself in an attempt to keep warm. If he was this cold inside a house with a heating system, albeit with the thermostat set on low, he couldn't imagine how brutal the cold must be outside -- especially for a small bird.

He turned back to the computer screen and focused on the technical problem.

The minutes slowly grew into an hour while he analyzed the problem and took steps to correct it. He was making progress, and he saw from the log file the error condition was improving.

Cold silence surrounded him in the low light and flicker of the computer screen. Most of the time the hum of the computer's fan and the clicking of the keyboard were the only sounds in the room, but every few minutes or so, as if on cue from some strange yet almost discernible schedule, the mournful cry again pierced the frozen air. Almost like clockwork, but the clock wasn't keeping exact time.

The sad sound tugged at Mark's heart. Somehow, almost intuitively, he picked up on the unseen bird's timing.

Just before the bird cried out the next time, Mark looked out into the darkness beyond the window. Just as he expected, the haunting call echoed through the night air.

As the minutes crept by, he timed the bird's cry almost exactly, working on the computer during the periods of silence and then pausing as he waited for the next mournful cry. He began to welcome the sound, because he knew each time he heard it that the bird was still alive. He hoped with all his heart that the bird could somehow survive until the morning, because if it did, the sun would warm the world once again. Maybe then this sad bird would eat and find the strength to live another day.

The cycle continued as time itself seemed to slow down and eventually lose its meaning in the predawn darkness.

Fatigue dulled his mind as he waited and watched the screen, his work now complete. All he had to do now was verify all was working and that it would remain that way.

"What are you doing?"

Mark jumped a few inches up out of his chair in shock at the unexpected voice.

His wife laughed a moment as she clutched her robe tighter. "I-I didn't mean to scare you, honey. I woke up, and you were gone."

"I got paged. I tried not to wake you when I got up." Mark sat down, his face warm with embarrassment.

Jane came over and hugged his shoulders as she looked at the screen with him. "Problem?"

"Yeah, but I think I got it licked."

"Coming back to bed?" She hugged his shoulders tighter, and her warmth sent a comforting glow through his body.

He hit the enter key and stood up. Now they put their arms around each other and hugged each other -- for affection as well as for warmth.

He leaned back and looked deep into Jane's brown eyes. "Hold me tight, pretty woman."

She tightened her embrace. "Hold me closer -- I'm cold too," she whispered.

"Anything you say."

They held each other a long time, the warmth of their bodies mingling delightfully.

Mark nestled his cheek against hers and then kissed her neck. Jane laughed. He kissed her ear and then whispered in a low voice, "Me Tarzan, you Jane." He laughed knowingly.

"We can't do that now," Jane said with a playful lilt.

"Why not?" Mark asked with a comically disappointed tone.

"It's too cold!"

Suddenly, another mournful cry pierced the night, but now it seemed more like the wailing sigh of some lost soul calling out from the depths of despair. Painfully, the single note slowly faded into nothingness.

Jane's eyes widened with surprise. "What was that?"

"That's the saddest bird I've ever heard," Mark whispered.

"It sounds like it's crying -- like a pitiful wail."

"He's been calling out like that every few minutes since I've been up."

"Why does he cry like that?"

"I'm guessing he's cold. It's about eighteen degrees out there -- a killing cold."

"The sun will be rising in less than an hour. If

he hangs on a little longer, it's supposed to warm up well above freezing today," Jane said.

"That's what I've been hoping, that he'll hang on until daylight."

"Are you almost done? I guess you'll be going into work late today?"

"Yes. I fixed it a while back ... just verifying everything is running smoothly. I was just getting ready to log off and get some sleep before I go in later."

"Good. I'll go get the bed warm for you." Jane kissed him on the cheek and hurried out of the room.

Mark made one last check and logged out. As he got up, both cats rose up and scurried into the kitchen ahead of him. When he walked into the kitchen on his way to the hallway and the stairs, he found both cats sitting next to their food bowls and looking expectantly at him.

Every morning when he awoke, the first two things he did when he came down were feed the cats and fill their bowl with fresh water. With both the kitty babies happily eating, he'd next pour himself a cup a coffee. Otherwise, the cats would circle restlessly around him until he finally gave in and fed them.

He dipped a cup of food into each of their bowls. He heard their contented crunching as he walked upstairs to get a little sleep before he went into work.

"Daddy!"

Mark turned toward the panic-stricken cry.

Philip scurried across the kitchen and leapt into his arms. Mark picked him up and held him close. He felt the little boy trembling against him.

"What's the matter, baby?" Mark asked soothingly.

Philip leaned back and rubbed his eyes. "I had a bad dream, Daddy."

"What kind of dream?"

"I dreamed I was lost and couldn't find my way back home. I kept calling for you and Mommy, but you never came to find me, and... and I was scared!" Philip sobbed with the last word and fell against Mark's chest, crying softly.

"Now, now. It was just a bad dream, nothing real. See, I'm right here holding you, and Mommy is upstairs sleeping. We're all here."

In the early morning twilight, Mark held his son close within his tender embrace. As the little boy's sobs slowly faded away, Mark hummed a tune to soothe the child into restfulness, much as he had rocked and hummed Philip to sleep as a tiny infant not so long ago. As he stood there, it almost seemed as if the bond of love between them had grown into something real, something that held them together just as real as their arms around each other.

"I --I was so afraid you and Mom were gone and I'd never see you again."

"Don't worry, buddy boy. I'm not going anywhere. Let's take you back to bed; it's still too early for little boys to be up."

"Could you sit on my bed until I go back to

sleep? Please, Dad. Please!" Philip pleaded with big eyes.

"Sure, I'll stay with you as long as you like."

Mark ascended the stairs holding his son tightly. He walked into the darkened bedroom, settled Philip in his bed, and gently tucked the covers around the little boy's face. Philip beamed a smile at his daddy.

"Close your eyes."

Philip closed his eyes while Mark held his hand, and just like before, Mark hummed a little tune by Mozart until Philip's eyes fluttered and finally closed. After a few minutes, the boy's even breathing and peaceful expression spoke of his entry into restful sleep.

Mark waited, cherishing the gentle silence while he watched his son sleeping. He sat there a long time, gently gazing at the cherubic face highlighted by the gradually brightening sky outside the window.

No treasure in the entire world could match the emotions that warmed his heart in those precious moments alone with his sleeping son.

He stifled a yawn and realized he'd better get into bed if he wanted to get a couple of hours sleep and still make it to work before mid-day.

When he reached the hallway he looked out the window and noticed the sky just beginning to lighten, heralding the coming sunrise. As he watched, he heard the haunting cry of the grief-stricken bird pierce the air one last time. Turning toward the window, Mark whispered urgently to the unseen creature, almost as if his words would really be heard.

"Hang on, little bird. A new day is almost here..."

to be continued
in book two of the trilogy
'Song of Life'
The Journey